ALSO BY RICHARD PAUL EVANS

The Walk
The Christmas List
Grace
The Gift
Finding Noel
The Sunflower
A Perfect Day
The Last Promise
The Christmas Box Miracle
The Carousel
The Looking Glass
The Locket
The Letter
Timepiece
The Christmas Box

For Children
The Dance
The Christmas Candle
The Spyglass
The Tower
The Light of Christmas

✴ RICHARD PAUL EVANS ✴

Promise Me

SIMON & SCHUSTER
NEW YORK   LONDON   TORONTO   SYDNEY

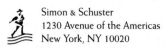

Simon & Schuster
1230 Avenue of the Americas
New York, NY 10020

Copyright © 2010 by Richard Paul Evans

First Simon & Schuster hardcover edition October 2010

SIMON & SCHUSTER and colophon are registered trademarks
of Simon & Schuster, Inc.

For information about special discounts for bulk purchases,
please contact Simon & Schuster Special Sales at
1-866-506-1949 or business@simonandschuster.com.

The Simon & Schuster Speakers Bureau can bring authors
to your live event. For more information or to book an event,
contact the Simon & Schuster Speakers Bureau at
1-866-248-3049 or visit our website at www.simonspeakers.com.

Designed by Davina Mock-Maniscalco

Manufactured in the United States of America

1 3 5 7 9 10 8 6 4 2

Library of Congress Cataloging-in-Publication Data

Evans, Richard Paul.
Promise me / Richard Paul Evans.
        p.   cm.
1. Single mothers—Fiction.   2. Guardian angels—Fiction.   I. Title.
PS3555.V259P76 2010

813'.54—dc22   2010027536

ISBN 978-1-4391-5003-0
ISBN 978-1-4391-5406-9 (ebook)

✦ ACKNOWLEDGMENTS ✦

*L*aurie Liss. Amanda Murray. (It was fun while it lasted, Amanda. Thank you for your insight and faith in this story. I really enjoyed working with you.) David Rosenthal. (David, it was a pleasure working with you for all these years, I wish you well in your new pursuits.) Carolyn Reidy. Gypsy da Silva. Copy editor Fred Wiemer. Jonathan Karp (I look forward to working with you, Jonathan). My writing assistant, Jenna Evans Welch.

For research assistance: Dr. David Benton (A terrific doctor. Thanks for always being there for me, David) and Kristy Benton. Mallorie Resendez Bassetti.

The staff: Barry James Evans, Diane Glad, Heather McVey, Judy Schiffman, Karen Christoffersen, Lisa V. Johnson,

Acknowledgments

Karen Roylance, Lisa McDonald, Sherri Engar, Doug Smith and Barbara Thompson.

Keri, Jenna and David Welch, Allyson-Danica, Abigail Hope, McKenna Denece, Michael. (Sorry, Bello. You were no help at all.)

My love and appreciation to all of you.

To Keri

Promise Me

PROLOGUE

*Locked away in jewelry boxes, hidden in my closet,
are two necklaces. They are gifts from two different men.
Both of these necklaces are beautiful, both of them
are valuable and I wear neither of them, but for entirely
different reasons—one because of a promise broken,
the other because of a promise kept.*

*As you read my story, there is something I want you to
understand. That in spite of all the pain—past, present
and that still to come—I wouldn't have done anything
differently. Nor would I trade the time I had with him for
anything—except for what, in the end, I traded it for.*

✴ Beth Cardall's Diary ✴

When I was a little girl, my mother told me that everyone has a secret. I suppose she was right. My name is Beth and this is the story of my secret. This is not where my story begins. Nor is this where it ends. This is, hopefully, where it is fulfilled.

It is Christmas Eve of 2008. The evening sky is flocked with wisps of snowflakes that meander indecisively from the sky like the floating seeds of cottonwoods. Our beautiful home in the canyon is aglow, lit in golden hues and decorated both inside and out for the season. It is cozy inside. There is a blazing flame in the living room fireplace beneath a dated family portrait, and a carved, wooden mantel crowded with our collection of German Steinbach Nutcrackers.

The smell of pine needles, scented candles and wassail fills the house along with the smells of Kevin's cooking. Kevin is my husband and on Christmas Eve it is *his* kitchen—a tradition begun seven Christmases ago that hopefully will never end.

The sweet, familiar peace of Christmas hymns provide a soundtrack to the evening. Everything is in place. Everything is perfect. It has to be. I've waited eighteen years for this night.

We are waiting to be joined by our evening's guests, our old friends Roxanne and Ray Coates, and our daughter Charlotte and her husband.

While Kevin finishes the last of his preparations, I'm upstairs in the master bathroom trying to compose myself, hoping that no one will notice that I've been crying.

Alone with my thoughts, I take down an old, cedar jewelry box from the top back shelf of my closet. I don't remember how long it's been since I've opened the box, but it is covered with dust. I set it on the bathroom counter and pull back its lid to expose the crushed red velvet interior and the single piece of jewelry inside—a delicate cameo pendant with the profile of an elegant woman carved into shell. The image is set in a gold bezel on a fine gold chain. I lift the necklace from the box. It's been many years since I've looked at it—many more since he gave it to me. There's a reason I don't wear the necklace. It holds so many feelings it would be like carrying an anvil around my neck. Already, just looking at it, I feel that weight as it opens a part of my mind I have kept closed: the evening in Capri when he kissed me and softly draped it around my neck. It was a different time, a different world, but the tears fall down my cheeks now just as they did then.

I fasten the necklace and look at myself in the mirror. I'm much older than I was the first time I wore it. It's hard to believe that eighteen years have passed.

For all those years I have carried a secret that I couldn't

share with anyone. No one would believe me if I told them. No one would understand. No one except the man I share my secret with. For eighteen years even he hasn't remembered. Tonight that may change. Tonight time has caught up to itself. I know this doesn't make sense to you now, but it will.

My story actually began in 1989. There are years of our lives that come and go and barely leave an imprint, but, for me, 1989 wasn't one of them. It was a hard year, and by hard I don't mean a day at the DMV, I mean *Siberian Winter hard*, one I barely survived and would never forget, as much as I wanted to.

It was the end of a decade and an era. It was a year of contrasts, of *Field of Dreams* and *Satanic Verses*. There were remarkable historic events that closed out the decade— the falling of the Berlin Wall and the Tiananmen Square massacre. There were a few notable passings as well: Lucille Ball, Bette Davis, and Irving Berlin died. My first husband, Marc, died as well, but that's all I'll say about that now. You'll understand why later.

I have loved three men in my life. I was married to Marc for seven years and I've been married to Kevin for twelve. But there was a man in between—a man I will always love— but a love that could never be. It was a little more than two months after Marc's death, on Christmas Day, that he came into my life and changed nearly every reality of my existence. How he came into my life and where he went is not easy to explain, but I'll do my best.

I've heard it said that reality is nothing but a collective dream. My story may challenge what you believe about heaven and earth. Or not. The truth is, you probably won't believe my story. I don't blame you. In the last eighteen years I've had plenty of time to think this over and honestly, had I not experienced it myself, I'm pretty certain that I wouldn't believe it either.

No matter. Tonight the silence may end. Tonight someone may share the secret with me, and even if no one else will ever know or believe what I've lived through, it's enough that I don't have to carry this alone. Maybe. Tonight, in just a few hours, I'll know for sure.

CHAPTER

One

There are days that live in infamy, for individuals as well as nations. February 12, 1989, was my personal equivalent of Pearl Harbor Day or September 11.

✦ Beth Cardall's Diary ✦

My life was never perfect, but up until February 12, it was pretty darn close. At least I thought it was. My husband Marc had been out of town for several weeks and had arrived home at around three in the morning. I heard him come into our room, undress and climb into bed. I rolled over, kissed him and put my arms around him. "I'm glad you're home."

"Me too."

I wasn't really cut out to be a salesman's wife. My idea of marriage is someone to share the weekdays with as well as the weekends. Most of all I hate sleeping alone. You would think that after five years I would have gotten used to it, but I hadn't. I never did.

Marc was still asleep when the radio-alarm went off three and a half hours later. I shut off the alarm, rolled over and held to his warm body for a few minutes, then kissed him on the neck and climbed out of bed. I got myself ready for the day, then woke our six-year-old daughter Charlotte, made her breakfast and drove her to school.

It was a routine I had grown accustomed to over the last six months, ever since Charlotte started the first grade and

I went back to work. With Marc on the road more often than not, I had become rather independent in my routine. I dropped Charlotte off at school, then went straight to my job at Prompt Cleaners—a dry cleaner about a mile and a half from our home in Holladay, Utah.

Marc made enough for us to live on, though not by much, and money was always tight. I worked to build us a financial cushion and for extras, as well as to get myself out of the house when Charlotte was at school. I'm not really a career gal, and I doubt working at a dry cleaner qualifies as such, but being cooped up in the house all day alone always made me a little crazy.

I had been at work a little over an hour and was in the back pressing suits when Roxanne came back to call me to the phone. She waved at me to get my attention. "Beth, it's for you. It's Charlotte's school."

Roxanne—or Rox, as she liked to be called—was my best friend at work. Actually, she was my best friend anywhere. She was thirty-eight, ten years older than I, small, five feet one, pencil-skinny and looked a little like Pat Benatar—whom you wouldn't know if you didn't do the eighties. She was from a small southern Utah town called Hurricane (pronounced Hurr-i-cun by the locals), and she spoke with a Hurricane accent, a slight, excited drawl, and used terms of endearment like rappers use curse words and with nearly the same frequency.

She'd been married for eighteen years to Ray, a short, barrel-chested man who worked for the phone company and sometimes moonlighted at a guard shack in a condominium development. She had one child, Jan, who was a blond, sixteen-year-old version of her mother. Jan was also Charlotte's and my favorite babysitter.

I love Roxanne. She's one of those people heaven too infrequently sends to earth—a joyful combination of lunacy and grace. She was my friend, sage, comic relief, confidante, Prozac and guardian angel all rolled up into one tight little frame. Everyone should have a friend like Roxanne.

"You heard me, darlin'?" she repeated. "Phone."

"Got it," I shouted over the hiss of the steam press. I hung up the jacket I was working on, then walked up front. "It's the school?"

Roxanne handed me the phone. "That's what the lady said."

I pulled back my hair and put the receiver to my ear. "Hello, this is Beth."

A young, female voice said, "Mrs. Cardall, this is Angela, I'm the school nurse at Hugo Reid Elementary. Your little Charlotte has been complaining of headaches and an upset stomach. She's here in my room lying down. I think she probably needs to come home."

I was surprised, as Charlotte was feeling perfectly fine an hour earlier when I dropped her off. "Okay. Sure. I'm at work right now, but my husband's home. One of us will be there within a half hour. May I talk to Charlotte?"

"Of course."

A moment later Charlotte's voice came softly from the phone. "Mommy?"

"Hi, sweetheart."

"I don't feel good."

"I'm sorry, honey. Daddy or I will come get you. We'll be there soon."

"Okay."

"I love you, sweetheart."

"I love you too, Mommy. Bye."

I hung up the phone. Roxanne looked over at me from the cash register. "Is everything okay?"

"Charlotte's sick. Fortunately, Marc's home."

I dialed the house and let the phone ring at least a dozen times before I finally gave up. I groaned, looked at Roxanne and shook my head.

"Not home?" Roxanne asked.

"That or he's still sleeping. I need to pick up Charlotte. Can you cover for me?"

"Can do."

"I don't know what's going on with Marc's schedule. I might not make it back."

"Don't worry about it. It's gonna be a slow day."

"Thanks. I owe you one."

"You owe me a lot more than one, sister," she said wryly. "And someday I'm gonna collect."

Charlotte's elementary school was only six blocks from the dry cleaner, just a few minutes by car. I parked my old Nissan in front of the school and walked to the office. The school secretary was expecting me and led me back to the nurse's office. The small, square room was purposely dim, lit only by a desk lamp. Charlotte was lying on a cot with her eyes closed, and the nurse was seated next to her. I walked up to the side of the cot, stooped over and kissed Charlotte's forehead. "Hi, honey."

Charlotte's eyes opened slowly. "Hi, Mommy." Her words were a little slurred and her breath had the pungent smell of vomit.

The nurse said, "I'm Angela. You have a sweet little girl here. I'm sorry she doesn't feel well."

"Thank you. It's peculiar, she was fine this morning."

"Miss Rossi said that she seemed okay when she arrived but started complaining of a headache and stomachache around ten. I took her temperature a half-hour ago but it was normal: 98.3."

I shook my head again. "Peculiar."

"It could be a migraine," she said. "That would explain the nausea. She threw up about ten minutes ago."

I rubbed Charlotte's cheek. "Oh, baby." I looked back. "She's never had a migraine before. Maybe a little rest will help. Thank you."

"Don't mention it. I'll let Miss Rossi know that she's gone home for the day."

I crouched down next to Charlotte. "Ready to go, honey?"
"Uh-huh."

I lifted her into my arms, then carried her, clinging to my shoulders, out to the car. She didn't say much as I drove home, and every time I glanced over at her, I was surprised by how sick she looked. I pulled into the driveway hoping that

Marc was still home, but his car was gone. I carried Charlotte inside and lay her in our bed. She was still lethargic. "Do you need anything, honey?"

"No." She rolled over to her stomach, burrowing her head into my pillow. I pulled the sheets up to her neck. I walked out of the room and tried Marc's office extension but only got his voicemail. I called Roxanne to let her know that it didn't look like I would be back to work today.

"Don't worry, baby," she said. "I've got your back."

"I love you," I said.

"Me too. Give Char a kiss for me."

Charlotte lay in bed the rest of the afternoon, sleeping away most of it. Around one I gave her some toast and 7-Up. A half-hour later she threw up again, then curled up in a ball complaining of a stomachache. I sat on the bed next to her, rubbing her back. For dinner I made homemade chicken noodle soup, which she managed to keep down.

Marc didn't get home until after seven. "Hey, babe," he said. "How was your day?"

I guess I needed someone to take the day's anxiety out on. "Awful," I said sharply. "Where have you been?"

He looked at me curiously, no doubt wondering what he'd done wrong. "You know how it is when I get back in town, it's one meeting after another."

"I tried your extension."

"Like I said, I was in meetings. If I had known you were

trying to reach me . . ." He put his arms around me. "But I'm here now. How about I take you and Char out for dinner?"

My voice softened. "Sorry, it's been a hard day. Charlotte's not feeling well. I had to pick her up from school. And I already made chicken noodle soup for dinner."

He leaned back, his concern evident on his face. "She's sick? Where is she?"

"In our bed."

He immediately went to see her. I turned on the burner beneath the soup, then followed Marc to our bedroom. Charlotte squealed when she saw him. "Daddy!"

He sat on the bed next to her. "How's my monkey?"

"I'm not a monkey."

"You're my monkey. You're my little baboon." He lay down next to her, his face close to hers. "Mommy says you're not feeling well."

"I have a tummy ache."

He kissed her forehead. "It's probably from eating all those bananas."

"I'm not a monkey!" she said again happily.

I couldn't help but smile. It was good to see her happy again. Charlotte adored Marc and missed him terribly when he was gone, which was at least two weeks out of every month. To his credit, Marc always did his best to be with us. He called every night to ask about my day and say goodnight to Charlotte.

"Did you eat dinner?"

"Mommy made me chicken soup."

"Was it good?"

She nodded.

"I think I'm going to get myself some soup if you didn't eat it all." He raised his eyebrow. "Did you eat it all, you little piggy?"

She laughed. "You said I was a monkey."

"That's right. So you stay in your bed and don't climb any more trees."

She giggled again. "I'm not a monkey!"

"I'm just making sure." Marc kissed her forehead, then got up and walked out of our bedroom, gently shutting the door behind him. "What's wrong with her? She looks like she's lost weight."

"I don't know. She came down with a headache then threw up at school."

"Does she have a fever?"

"No. It's probably just a little migraine or something. It will probably be gone by tomorrow." I put my arms around him. "I'm glad you're home finally."

"Me too." He kissed me. "More than you know." Then he kissed me again. We kissed for several minutes.

I pushed him back. "You did miss me," I said playfully.

"So, is the little one sleeping in our bed tonight?"

I knew why he was asking and it made me happy. "No. She'll be sleeping in her own bed."

"Good. I've missed you."

"I've missed you too," I said. "I hate a cold bed."

"Me too." He kissed me one more time, then stepped back. "So you made soup?"

I brushed the hair back from my face. "Yes. It should be hot by now. Would you like some bread? I baked one of those frozen loaves."

"I would love some."

We walked back to the kitchen. Marc sat down at the table and I went to the stove. The soup was lightly bubbling. I turned the stove off, then ladled him a bowl. "So how was Phoenix? Or was it Tucson?"

"Both. They were both good. The economy's hot right now, so these hospitals are pretty loose with their budgets. And the weather in Arizona is fantastic, blue skies and in the seventies."

"I wish it was here. You shouldn't have to breathe air you can see."

"Yeah, I had a coughing fit the moment I entered the valley. We need a good snowstorm to clear it out."

Around February the snow in Salt Lake is as dirty and gray as the underside of an automobile, and, too often, so is the air. The Salt Lake Valley is surrounded by the Rocky Mountains to the east and the Oquirrh Mountains to the west, so when a winter low-pressure front moves in, the pollution is caught inside until a big storm blows it out.

"I wonder if I'm coming down with something like Charlotte. Yesterday I got up early to work out, but I didn't have any energy. I ended up going back to bed."

"You're probably not getting enough sleep. What time did you come in this morning?"

"Around three."

"I really wish you wouldn't drive so late. It's not safe." I set the bowl of soup and a thick slice of warm bread in front of Marc. "Do you want butter for your bread?"

"Yes. And honey, please."

I fetched the butter dish and a plastic honey bear bottle from the cupboard and set them both on the table next to Marc, then I sat down next to him at the table, my elbows on the table and my chin in my hands. "If Charlotte's sick tomorrow, can I leave her home with you?"

"I can't in the morning. We've got a company sales meeting at nine, then afterwards I'm meeting with Dean to try to keep him from cutting my territory."

"How about the afternoon?"

"I can pull that off." He squeezed some honey onto his buttered bread. "Do you think she'll still be sick?"

"Probably not. But just in case."

He took a bite of his bread, then followed it with a spoonful of soup.

"How's the soup?" I asked.

"You make the best chicken noodle soup I know. It's almost worth getting sick for."

I smiled at the compliment. "Thanks."

"So how are things going at the cleaners?"

"Same-old same-old."

"Rox been committed yet?"

"Not yet. But they'll eventually catch up with her."

"You know, all this traveling isn't getting any easier," he said. "It's lonely on the road. I really missed you this time."

"Me too. I hate the life of the wife of a traveling salesman."

"That sounds like a country song," he said. "Or an Arthur Miller play."

"I hope not. At least the latter."

He smiled and took another bite of soup. "Me too. The latter."

CHAPTER

Two

Sufficient to the day is the evil thereof.
I used to wonder what that meant. I wish I still did.

✦ Beth Cardall's Diary ✦

The next morning Marc got up, kissed me on the cheek, rolled out of bed and was gone. About an hour later I pulled on my robe, then went to check on Charlotte. She was still sleeping. I opened her blinds halfway, then sat on the bed next to her. "Charlotte," I said.

She groaned as she rolled over. She put her hand on her head and started to cry.

"Do you still hurt?"

"My head hurts," she said. I put my cheek on her forehead but she was cool.

"How's your tummy?"

"It hurts too."

I rubbed her back. "Is it better or worse than yesterday?"

"It's more bad," she said.

I leaned over and kissed her head. "You go back to sleep, okay?" I pulled the covers back up to her chin, shut her blinds, then went to get ready for the day. I called our pediatrician, Dr. Benton, and made an appointment for a quarter to noon. Then I called Roxanne.

"Hey, girl, I can't come in this morning. Charlotte's still really sick."

Roxanne grunted. "You know that nasty flu bug is going around. Yesterday, Jan stayed home from school with it."

"I don't think it's the flu. She doesn't have a temperature. I'm taking her in to the doctor's this morning."

"Let me know what he says. I'll ask Teresa if she can come in early."

"Thanks. Marc says he'll be home this afternoon, so if you want I can come in around two or so and work the evening shift."

"That's better. I'm sure Teresa would love to switch shifts. She's young and still has a night life."

Around ten-thirty I carried Charlotte into the kitchen and made her some breakfast—oatmeal with brown sugar. She didn't want to eat, so I laid her on the couch, where she could watch *Sesame Street* while I got ready for the day. A little before noon I took Charlotte to our pediatrician, Dr. Dave Benton. We had been seeing Dr. Benton since Charlotte was only six weeks old and colicky, so we had a pretty good patient-doctor thing going.

The clinic was packed. When the inversion settles into the valley, there's always a lot of sickness, and the waiting room was as crowded as a Macy's on Black Friday. It took us more than an hour to see the doctor, for which he was apologetic.

"I'm sorry, Beth," he said, looking a little run-down himself. "It's like Grand Central Station around here. It seems like half the valley is sick, and the other half has a cough. So what's up with our princess?"

"She came home early from school yesterday with a head-ache and stomach pains. She's thrown up three times."

He smiled at Charlotte as he reached out to feel her neck. "Well, let's see if we can find out what's going on."

"My dad says it's because I eat too many bananas," Charlotte said. "He says I'm a monkey."

He smiled. "You're not as hairy as most of the monkeys I've seen, but I'll keep that in mind. Charlotte, could you take off your glasses for me so I can check your eyes?"

Charlotte took off her pink-rimmed glasses and opened her eyes wide as the doctor shone a light into one, then the other. He then ran through the usual examination of her vitals.

"Huh," he said, rubbing his chin. "No cough, no swelling and no fever. I don't know what to tell you, Beth. She's dropped a couple pounds since her last visit, and her face looks a little puffy, like she's been retaining water. But other than that and how she feels, everything seems to be fine." He looked at Charlotte. "Does your head still hurt?"

She nodded.

He turned back to me. "Does she have any allergies?"

"Not that I've noticed."

"It could be a little virus. For now, I'd give her some children's Tylenol for her headache and keep her home. If she's not doing any better in a few days, you might have to take her up to Primary Children's Medical Center for some additional testing."

I didn't like the sound of that. "All right. Thanks."

"I wish I could tell you more."

"Maybe it's nothing." I looked down at Charlotte. She looked exhausted. "Ready to go, honey?"

"Yes."

I took her in my arms. "Thanks again, Doctor."

"You're welcome. Keep us informed."

As I drove home, a subtle dread settled over me. I'm not a hypochondriac—for me or my family—but something was wrong. I could feel it. Sometimes a mother just has a sense about these things. I honked as I pulled into our driveway. Marc met me at the front door and took Charlotte from me. She clung to him, burying her head in his neck.

"What did the doctor say?" he asked.

"He doesn't know what's wrong. He said if she's still sick in a few days we should take her to the hospital for tests."

"The hospital?"

"Just for tests. But we'll wait until Saturday."

"Saturday is Valentine's Day," Marc said.

I looked at him blankly. In seven years of marriage we'd never done anything on Valentine's Day. Frankly, Marc was about as romantic as a tennis shoe, and called Valentine's Day "a conspiracy by florists and candy makers to fatten their wallets."

"I made us dinner reservations at the Five Alls."

"How did you get us reservations on Valentine's Day?"

"I made them three months ago."

The Five Alls was my favorite restaurant. It's also where Marc and I got engaged.

"Should I cancel the reservation?"

I rubbed Charlotte's back. "Let's see how she's doing. When do you leave town next?"

"I'm in Scottsdale next Tuesday. There's a medical conference at the Phoenician resort. Want to come?"

"I have a sick six-year-old and a job. In what fictional world would that be possible?"

He grinned. "I know. Sometimes it's just nice to be asked. So are you off to work now?"

"Yes. I've missed too many days lately. I hope Arthur doesn't decide to fire me."

"He can't live without you."

"Yeah, right. He can't even get my name right. Half the time he calls me Betty. I better go. See you." I kissed him, then Charlotte. "See you, honey."

"Bye, Mommy."

As I stepped off the porch, Marc said, "Oh, would you mind taking in my laundry and dry cleaning? Everything's in the back seat of my car. It's unlocked."

"Sure."

"And tell Phil he used so much starch on my shirts last time I could slice bread with my sleeve."

"Phil doesn't do the shirts," I said. "I'll tell the girls to back off a little. See you tonight."

"I'll order some pizza. We can have a quiet night at home."

"I don't think Charlotte's stomach can handle pizza."

"I want pizza," she said.

I shook my head. "Of course you do."

"Sorry," Marc said. "See you."

Marc carried Charlotte inside. I grabbed his laundry out of his car, threw it on my back seat, then drove into work.

Prompt Dry Cleaners was housed in a cinder-block-walled, box-shaped yellow building off Highland Drive in Holladay, next to a Baskin-Robbins. It was a small, family-owned business established in 1944 by the Huish family, but the only Huish that still worked there—and I use the word 'work' loosely—was Arthur, the general manager, who looked like he was eighty or ninety and rarely came around the cleaners because in his words, the chemical smells made his sinuses "coagulate."

There were six employees in all—the serfs, we called ourselves—me, Roxanne, Teresa, Jillyn, Emily and Phil, the lone male, who ran the dry-cleaning machine. Our positions, with the exception of Phil's, were interchangeable, though I usually worked the buck steam press in back, which gave me a little more flexibility with my hours.

Roxanne was acting manager when Arthur wasn't around, which was nearly always, so I considered her my boss. She was working the front counter when I walked in, my arms overflowing with Marc's laundry.

"You're new here, aren't you?" she said sardonically. "May I help you?"

"I'm beyond help," I said.

"You got that right, sister. How's my Char-baby?"

"Still sick. Marc has her." I dropped the laundry on the counter. "Thanks again for filling in."

"No *problem-o*."

I filled out a laundry slip then, as usual, started going through the pockets of Marc's clothes, looking for pens and secretly hoping for money.

"I'll get it," Roxanne said. "We're a little backed up on the pressing, if you don't mind."

"No *problem-o*," I replied. "I'm on it." I walked on back to the press.

The back of the cleaners was as austere as a car wash—windowless, with painted cinder-block walls—and just as noisy; a symphony of steam and pneumatic blasts in a jungle of pipe and rails. (If you close your eyes, the noise of the presses resembles that of an amusement park ride.) We always kept a fan going in the back, even in winter, because the smell of perchloroethylene, the cleaning fluid used in the dry-cleaning machine, saturated the air. It took me a few weeks to get used to it, but after a while I began to like it.

Phil had an ancient radio and as usual it was blaring country music. (We joked with him that his radio was so old it only got fifties music.) The steam press I usually operated was near the dry-cleaning machine where Phil was working. He turned down the music and waved at me. "How's it goin', Beth?"

"Good. How are you, Phil?"

"Can't complain. Well, I could, but it wouldn't do no good, would it?" He laughed.

I smiled. "Probably not."

I liked Phil. He was a balding, soft-spoken, middle-aged man, and a Vietnam vet. My first day on the job Roxanne told me that he had been a POW for the last five months of the war, before Nixon negotiated the prisoners' release. He was a hard worker and friendly, but kept very much to himself. I wondered what he was like before the war. He was always kind to me, and always had a Tootsie Pop for Charlotte whenever I brought her in. Every morning he welcomed me with the same greeting and laughed just as hard afterward as he had the first time he said it. I'd miss it if he didn't.

"Have a good day," he said, disappearing back into the labyrinth of clothing.

"You too, Phil," I said.

There were three full racks of suit coats and trousers at my station waiting to be pressed. I had pulled a rack close to the press and started pressing when Roxanne came toward me. She was walking quickly, shaking her head. "Honey, it's not good," she said as she neared, "not good."

I looked at her quizzically. "What's not good?"

"I found this in Marc's suit." She handed me a piece of paper—a handwritten note. The penmanship was light and feminine.

Hey, Gorgeous Man,

I missed you while you were gone. It's cold in Utah without you. Brrrr! You need to come warm me up! Thank you for the

Valentine's gift, you know we girls are like birds, we just love shiny things. Can't wait to thank you properly in sunny Scottsdale. I'll bring something tiny to wear just for you.

Heart you,
Ash

There was a smudged crimson lipstick kiss at the bottom of the note.

My heart, my lungs, the whole world, froze. Then I began to tremble. "He's cheating on me."

"I'm sorry," Roxanne said, looking pale. "Maybe it's . . ." she stopped. There was no other explanation.

"He's going to Scottsdale on Tuesday." I looked up at her blankly. "We're so happy. Why would he . . ." My eyes filled with tears.

"Baby." She put her arms around me. "That stupid, bone-headed creep," she said. "A gorgeous feast like you at home and he goes dumpster-diving."

My head was spinning and I felt light-headed, like I might faint.

"Sit down," Roxanne said. "Breathe." She pushed a chair toward me. "Here, breathe, honey."

I sat as everything around me spun. After a while, I don't know how long, I said, "I've got to go. I'm sorry. I've got to go."

"Honey, be careful. Let me drive you."

"I just need to go." I stood and walked outside to my car. Roxanne followed me out. "Baby, don't do anything crazy. What are you going to do? Tell me what you're going to do."

"I'm going to talk to my husband."

˚✦˚

The drive home was a blur. That stupid note lay open on the seat next to me. Every time I looked at it, the lipstick kiss seemed to jump off the paper at me, sharp as a slap. I felt so humiliated. So small. So stupid.

At one red light I completely melted down, sobbing, until the car behind me laid on the horn.

Five minutes later I screeched into our driveway. Shaking, I walked into the house. Maybe you're supposed to rehearse these things, but I had no idea what I was going to say. Marc was sitting on the couch next to Charlotte reading her a book. He looked up at me as I entered the room. "Hey, you're back early," he said smiling. His expression changed when he saw my tear-swollen face. "What's wrong?"

"Who is she?"

"Wha . . ."

I held up the note. "Who is *she*?"

He looked stricken, like one of those guys on a *Dateline* sting who's just been caught on camera. He glanced down at Charlotte, then back at me and stood up. "Come here," he said to me. "Charlotte doesn't need to hear this."

"Where you going, Daddy?" Charlotte asked.

"Daddy and Mommy need to talk," he said.

I followed him into our bedroom. I was trembling with all the emotions that were flowing through me. "Who is she?"

He took a deep breath. "She works up in Ogden. She's a supply manager for St. Jude's recover—"

I screamed, "I don't care about her résumé! Who is she?"

He rubbed the back of his neck. "She's a woman I met a while back. We've been . . . seeing each other."

"How long have you been sleeping with her?"

"I'm not sure. Maybe six months."

"You're not sure." I tried to maintain my composure. "Why? Why would you do that?"

He just stood there looking dumb.

"You need to go. You need to leave this house."

"Beth." He reached out for me. "Honey—"

"Don't touch me. Don't call me honey. Don't say my name. You need to go."

"She doesn't mean anything to me."

I began to cry again. "Well, she means a lot to me."

Just then our bedroom door opened. "Daddy?"

"Not now, Charlotte," I said.

". . . I threw up."

"Get out," I said to Marc.

"Come on, Beth." He again took a step toward me, his arms extended.

"Don't touch me!" I screamed. "How could you do this to me?"

Charlotte started crying. "Stop yelling at Daddy!"

"Charlotte," Marc said. "I'll be out in a minute. Go back and watch TV." Charlotte took a few steps from the door, then stopped, frightened but too fearful to leave.

I put my hand over my eyes. I wanted to die. With all my heart I wanted to die. When I looked up, I said, "I thought we had a good marriage." My voice cracked, "I thought you loved me."

"Beth, I do love you. It's not . . ."

I looked at him. "It's not what?"

"It's not as bad as you think."

I stared at him in utter amazement. "How much worse could it be?"

"She's just a friend."

"This is what you do with your friends?"

"Please don't make this worse than it is. I was going to tell you. I've been trying to end this."

"You need to go. Go to your girlfriend, your . . . Ash, or whatever her stupid name is."

"I don't love her, Beth. I love *you*."

I slapped him. "How dare you say that! How dare you?" I started sobbing again.

"Daddy!" Charlotte screamed. "Don't hit Daddy."

"Charlotte," Marc said. "Go to your room now!"

My legs felt weak, like I might collapse. "Please go," I pleaded. "Please, just go away."

He exhaled deeply. "Okay." He took a few steps toward the door, then turned back. "It's not your fault," he said.

"Why would you even say that?"

"Because I know you. I know you'll blame yourself later. But don't." He walked outside of the bedroom, still within my view. "Come here, Char-char," he said. "Daddy's got to go away on another trip."

"I don't want you to go," she said, her voice cracking. "Please don't go."

"I'm sorry, honey, I have to. But I'll call. I promise."

She grabbed onto his legs and began to cry. "Is it because Mommy hit you?"

He crouched down, and wrapped his arms around her. "I have to go. And Mommy didn't do anything bad. Daddy was bad. And Mommy will be here for you. She'll take good care of you." I didn't know if Marc was talking to Charlotte or me. He kissed the top of her head. "I'll be back as soon as I can." I'm not sure why, but he looked back at me. I turned away. Marc kissed her again, then stood. "Be brave now. Go to Mommy."

She wiped her eyes. "Okay."

Marc stood and walked away. Charlotte came into the room and wrapped her arms around my legs. I knew I needed to be strong for Charlotte, but I failed miserably. I broke down crying as soon as I heard the front door shut. I couldn't help it. It was as if the ground had given in beneath me and I fell to my knees and wept. I kept asking myself the same question: *How could he do this to us?* I loved him. I would have loved him forever. I would have stayed with him forever. Our fairy-tale romance had burned to the ground. Ash was a fitting name for the other woman.

CHAPTER

Three

*Life is a house of cards, balanced on a teeter-totter,
precariously perched on a roller coaster.
The only thing that should surprise us about our
surprises is that we are surprised by them.*

✶ Beth Cardall's Diary ✶

Roxanne called the house several times that night, but I couldn't bring myself to answer the phone, so she took it on herself to come by around seven. She let herself in the front door and walked right into my bedroom. Charlotte was in the living room watching television. I was lying in my bed with the night-table lamp still on. I'm certain that my face was as puffy as a bag of marshmallows.

"Oh, baby," she said when she saw me. She sat on the bed next to me, her legs dangling from the side. "Are you okay?"

"I made him leave," I said hoarsely.

"Of course you did."

"Charlotte was so upset."

"You did the right thing."

"Charlotte's still sick."

Roxanne shook her head. "Baby, when it rains it pours. That's why you got me. I'm your umbrella and your galoshes." She gently ran her hand over my cheek. "I called Ray and told him I wouldn't be home tonight. What have you got for dinner?"

"I'm not hungry. Charlotte . . ."

"Don't worry about a thing, I'll make Charlotte a grilled

cheese, she loves those. Then I'll give her a bath and get her ready for bed. You just rest." She slid from the bed.

"Rox."

"Yeah, baby."

"Thank you."

"Whatever I can do, baby. That's what I do, whatever I can do."

CHAPTER

We still don't know what's wrong with Charlotte.
I'd like to cry a swimming pool,
but then I'd probably drown myself in it.

✶ Beth Cardall's Diary ✶

Roxanne stayed until midnight, maybe later, I'm not sure. She was there when I fell asleep. Charlotte slept in my bed with me. The next morning felt dark, even though there were finally blue skies. I felt like I had woken with a bag of concrete on my chest.

It was Valentine's Day, which felt like a cruel, cosmic joke. I couldn't imagine a greater irony. I rolled over and held Charlotte. She woke an hour or so later. I could see in her face that she still felt sick.

Roxanne had come in after Charlotte's bath and asked about a rash she'd found on her legs. The rash was something new. Oddly it gave me hope. Perhaps it might be a clue to what was wrong.

"I want Daddy," Charlotte said.

"I know." My eyes watered. "But will you be my Valentine?"

"And Daddy's."

I rubbed her cheek. "Do you still feel sick?"

"Yes."

I sighed. "I guess we're going to see some doctors today."

A half-hour later I forced myself out of bed. I wasn't hungry, but I hadn't eaten since lunch the day before and felt weak, so I made myself some coffee and toast, then got myself ready. As I put on my makeup, I started to cry again. I felt like I could cry a swimming pool. But I felt stronger than I had last night and stopped myself. I didn't have the luxury of collapse. Charlotte needed me.

I finished my makeup, doing my best to disguise my puffy eyes, then walked back into my bedroom to find that Charlotte had fallen back asleep. I woke her again, dressed her, then carried her out to the kitchen and made her cinnamon toast for breakfast. She didn't want to eat, but I insisted. She had already lost too much weight for me to let her skip meals. Then I drove her up to Primary Children's Medical Center. We sat in the waiting room for more than an hour before a nurse took us back to an examination room.

"How long has"—she looked down at the chart for a name—"Charlotte been ill?"

"Since Thursday. But I think she's been losing weight for the last few weeks."

"Is this the first time you've seen someone about it?"

"No, I saw my doctor a couple days ago. He told me to come see you if she hadn't improved by now."

"Could you go over the symptoms for me?"

"She's had an upset stomach with vomiting and diarrhea and stomach pains, as well as a bad headache. I've also noticed that she seems tired all the time. And she's losing weight."

"Has she had a fever?"

"No."

"And what about this rash?" Charlotte was wearing a knee-length skirt, and a patch of red bumps was clustered on her thighs and knees.

"We just noticed them last night. Do you think they're related?"

"Not necessarily. They could be caused by the weather. We see a lot of eczema during the winter months because everyone's skin gets so dry."

I don't know if the nurse noticed my disappointment, but she added, ". . . but we'll definitely want to take it into consideration. What are her eating habits?"

"What do you mean?"

"Is she a good eater, or is she finicky at meals?"

"Lately she hasn't been eating much."

She turned to Charlotte and touched her on the arm. "We're going to do a few tests just to get us on the right track and get you feeling better. Is that okay?"

Charlotte nodded. "Uh-huh."

She cried when the nurse slid a needle into her arm to take a blood sample. They also took a stool sample and a throat culture. Then we waited at the hospital for the results.

Two hours later a young male doctor came to see us. "Mrs. Cardall?"

"Yes."

"I'm Dr. Reese, it's nice to meet you. This is what we know so far. Charlotte's blood work shows that she has iron deficiency anemia. This can account for her fatigue, weakness, pale skin and headaches.

"Now, the question is, why is she anemic? You told the

nurse that she's been a poor eater lately. So we're thinking that in Charlotte's case it is possibly a dietary issue. Children who are picky eaters can become deficient in certain nutrients. I'd like to put her on some iron supplements as well as a high-iron diet. You'll need to make sure that she gets plenty of dairy products, eggs and meat."

I nodded, grateful for any diagnosis and open to any counsel. The doctor continued. "However, anemia is just one piece of the puzzle, and it doesn't account for all of her gastrointestinal issues. We're going to have a diagnostic meeting in the morning, so we'd like to keep her here overnight just to keep an eye on her."

"Overnight?" It's not that I wasn't willing to let her stay, I just didn't want what she had to be that bad.

"You're the mother, but we think it would be best."

Really there was nothing to do but submit. I called Roxanne from the hospital to let her know where I was. She told me that Marc had called the cleaners twice looking for me and asking for information on Charlotte. He left the phone number of the hotel where he was staying. Honestly, a part of me was glad to see him suffering too.

Later that evening I phoned him back. He was clearly surprised that I called. "Beth, I—"

I cut him off. "I didn't call for me. We're up at Primary Children's Medical Center, and Charlotte's been asking for you."

"Did they figure out what's wrong?"

"Not completely. She's severely anemic, but they're not sure why. They're keeping her here overnight to keep an eye on her."

"I'm sorry you're going through this alone," Marc said. "If you want, I'll come up and spell you off."

"That won't be necessary," I said curtly. "Here's your daughter." I handed the phone to Charlotte.

"Daddy!"

I watched her smile for the first time that day and it made me angry. I was the one at her side worrying over her. I felt like I did all the work and he got the pay. I feared that Charlotte blamed me for his not being there. It was so unfair. *I wasn't the bad guy here. I'm not the one who cheated.* Then why was I punishing myself as well? Why did I feel guilty for keeping him away? They talked for another five minutes before I took the phone back.

"Where is the hotel?" I asked.

"It's the Jolly Midas just off Seventy-second."

"Are you with *her*?"

"Her?" He was silent for a moment. "Of course not. I told her that I love you and I never wanted to see her again."

"You want an award for that?"

"Beth, I made a big mistake. There's no excuse for it. But most of all, I'm sorry that I hurt you. I know they're just words, but I mean it. There's no one in the world I care about more than you."

"Except yourself," I said.

"Yeah, well, a couple days ago I might have agreed with you. But I know that's not true. Because right now I'm punishing myself more than you could. You're the only woman I've ever loved. I got what I deserve."

I sat quietly listening, my eyes filling with tears. "I've got to go," I said.

"Let me know what I can do to help. Anything. You don't have to forgive me to let me help."

"I'll think about it," I said, then hung up before he could respond.

I wiped my eyes. Charlotte was looking at me. "Why are you crying? Do you miss Daddy?"

I looked at her for a moment. "I guess I do."

She put her hand on mine. "It's okay, Mommy. He always comes home."

Everything in my life seemed in commotion—a dark and complex labyrinth that I not only didn't know how to navigate; I didn't even know where it led. That night I slept in a chair by Charlotte's side. I suppose, on some level, my concern for Charlotte helped keep me sane, as it was easier to forget my pain by focusing on hers.

The next morning around eleven, Dr. Reese came into the room. Charlotte was asleep, and I was sitting in a chair next to her reading *Good Housekeeping* magazine. The doctor motioned for me to step outside the room to talk.

"Mrs. Cardall, this morning we sat down as a diagnostic team and looked over all the test results. The bottom line is, we don't really know what's wrong with Charlotte. We don't believe it's parasites and we've cleared giardia infection as an option. What we know for certain is that her iron count is low, her growth seems to be stunted and that she is still losing weight."

My hope fell. "So what do we do?"

"There's a possibility that she's having some issues with her gallbladder, but before we send her to a gastroenterologist and make her go through even more tests, I'd like to start treating her for the iron deficiency and see if we can't clear up some of these issues. So in the meantime, I'm going to prescribe an iron supplement and I recommend plenty of liquids to keep her hydrated. We also recommend that you feed her more red meat. The natural iron will help."

"What if she doesn't get better?"

He rubbed his neck. "Then check back with us in a couple weeks."

I helped Charlotte get dressed, then we went downstairs. On the way out I stopped at the hospital's billing office to check out. I nearly drained my emergency checking account just paying my medical deductible. Then I carried Charlotte out to the car. I called Roxanne as soon as I got home.

"What do you know?" she asked.

"That I'm a thousand dollars poorer and Charlotte has an iron deficiency but we don't know why. Why can't anyone figure out what's going on?"

"Those doctors," she said angrily. "Don't get me started. They prescribed arthritis medicine for Ray for six months before we figured out he only had gout. So what are you supposed to do?"

"Give her more iron."

"What about school?"

"I'm going to keep her out a few more days, then try again."

"And work?" There was tension in her voice.

"I need to be home with Charlotte. What's going on?"

"Arthur suggested we start looking for a replacement."

"I can't lose my job."

"I know. I told him if he's thinking of replacing you, he can replace me as well."

"You shouldn't have done that."

"Yes, I should have. That old man can't bully us around. Besides, you think I want to spend my days listening to Teresa's exploits in Manworld? I'd rather stick darning needles in my ears."

"I can't let you lose your job. And I can't afford to lose mine. What do I do?"

"Can't Marc help?" she asked.

"He offered."

"You should let him help."

I groaned. "I just don't know if I can look at him."

"Well, you don't have to let him move back in. It's not about you, it's about Charlotte."

I exhaled slowly. "Maybe you're right. I need to think about it. Thanks for watching my back."

"That's what I do, babe."

CHAPTER

Five

Why do we delay the changes that will bring us happiness?
It's like finally fixing up the house
the week before you sell it.

✴ Beth Cardall's Diary ✴

Marc called around seven that night to talk to Charlotte. For the first time since I sent him away, I was glad to hear his voice. In all honesty, it was more than just exhaustion from going through all of this alone. I missed our family. And even as deeply as I'd been hurt, I missed *him*. But I wasn't about to tell him that.

"Hi, Beth," he said. "How are you?"

"Here's Charlotte," I said, handing her the phone. As usual, Charlotte was happy to hear his voice, and within just a few minutes she was laughing. As I watched her, I knew just how much she needed her father. After they had talked a while, I told Charlotte to say goodbye and give me back the phone. I put it up to my ear. "Marc, I need to talk to you."

"Okay," he said tentatively, "I'm listening."

"I need to go into the other room. Call back in a couple minutes."

"All right."

I hung up the phone, kissed Charlotte good night, then went to my bedroom. The phone rang as I was walking in. I picked it up and sat on the bed. "Hello."

"It's Marc."

"Listen, I don't want you to take this wrong. I'm just as angry and hurt as I was a couple days ago. Maybe even more. But this isn't a time to just be thinking about us. Right now our little girl is sick and she needs you. And I need your help. I can't do this alone. I've missed so much work lately that I may lose my job."

"You want me to come back home?" he asked.

"I don't *want* you to. But I think, with things the way they are, it would be best for Charlotte."

He was quiet for a moment. "When can I come back?"

"Tomorrow afternoon. Then I could work the late shift."

"I'll be back around lunchtime."

"I want to be very clear about this, Marc. You can't touch me and you're not sleeping in my bed. You can sleep in the front room on the couch. Are you clear on this?"

"It's for Charlotte," he said. "No touching."

"It's only for Charlotte," I repeated.

"Understood." We were both silent for a moment, then he said, "It will be good to see you."

"I'll see you tomorrow."

"Bye," he said.

As I hung up, my eyes welled up with tears. Beneath my veneer of anger I was soft. Part of me, a part of me that I despised at that moment, wanted to curl up in his arms and cry. I hated being so needy. I hated wanting healing from the man who had inflicted the injury.

The next day, Marc arrived at noon carrying a McDonald's bag. As he walked in the house, I thought he looked a little peaked, which was understandable for the emotional ride we'd been on. "I brought Charlotte something for lunch."

"I already made her a sandwich, but thanks. When do you leave town next?"

"Three weeks."

"Not for three weeks?"

"I told Dean to go ahead and change my territory like he wanted. It will cost us some commissions, but I won't need to be gone as much."

I couldn't believe the changes Marc was making. "That will be good," I said.

"Hold on. I got you something." He brought a long, narrow box out of his pocket and set it on the kitchen table next to me. "It's a . . ." He suddenly looked embarrassed. "Just open it."

I lifted the lid off the box. Inside was a beautiful strand of pearls. I had always wanted pearls.

"What is this for?" I asked.

"It's a late Valentine's Day present." Then more softly, "It's a *token of my love*."

I put the lid back on the box. Under different circumstances I would have squealed with delight. I would have thrown my arms around him, grateful for such a fabulous gift. But circumstances had changed. I knew that the pearls weren't a token of his love, they were a token of *what he'd done*. I knew I could never wear the necklace—it would only remind me of *her*. "Thanks," I said sadly. I left the box on the table and went to work.

CHAPTER

Six

Is it our actions or our desires that define us?
That's like asking if the trip is made by the horse
or the buggy.

✦ Beth Cardall's Diary ✦

Roxanne clapped enthusiastically when I walked in through the cleaners' front door. "I should have baked a cake," she said.

"Should have," I replied.

"So how's it going?" she asked, following me back to the press.

"Char's been doing a little better. I think she might be able to go back to school in a couple days."

"And how are things with Marc?"

I thought of the pearls. "I don't know. He just got back."

"But you've talked with him."

I looked up at her. "He's remorseful and humble and walking on eggshells. And part of me just wants to smack him. Why can't he have the decency to at least be a jerk? Then I could feel good about hating him."

"Well, don't kid yourself, he is a jerk and deserves to be smacked. Just don't get too carried away."

"What do you mean?"

"Simple math. If you really want your marriage over, then spare yourself the drama and cut loose. But that's not really what you want."

"How do you know that?"

"Because I know you better than you know yourself. You still love him. You wouldn't be so angry if you didn't. So if you're not going to end the thing, don't damage it any more than you have to. You can beat your car with a baseball bat for breaking down, but if you're not going to get rid of it, then someday you'll end up paying for all the damage you inflict. Does that make sense?"

I looked at her, wondering where she came up with this stuff. "In your usual twisted way, yes."

"I know it sounds strange to say it, but in some ways you're lucky. Everyone makes mistakes. Under the right circumstances even you might."

"I would never—"

She interrupted me. "Never say never, baby. Good people sometimes do bad things. But at least Marc is willing to own up to it and seek forgiveness. That says something about him. And he's been there for Charlotte all along. It's not easy for him to come crawling back into the lioness's den to take care of his daughter, but he's willing. He gets a gold star for that."

"You're saying he's a good guy?"

"I'm saying that he's human. And to err is human. To forgive . . . well, that's love."

CHAPTER

Seven

Hate, resentment and anger are parasites that feed off the heart until there's nothing left for love to live on.

✦ Beth Cardall's Diary ✦

Over the next few weeks Charlotte's health remained about the same, except I was having more trouble getting her to eat and she was still losing weight.

Ironically, I hadn't had Marc around the house that much since we first got married. It's like I had to get rid of him to get him back. He seemed changed in other ways. He seemed more of a homebody, as if his previous ambition had drained from him. He even started going to bed early. I asked him if he was all right, but he just shrugged. "It's just a hard time," he said.

As things fell back into a natural rhythm, I found myself mulling over what Roxanne had said about beating the car. She was right about one thing. I still loved Marc. That's why his cheating hurt so much.

Forgiveness requires selective memory, and after several weeks I decided to move his dalliance from center stage. His sin may not have been forgotten, but it wasn't dictating our every interaction either. I began to see the man I loved again.

Five weeks after he had moved back in, I decided to make a change. I was sitting in the break room eating my lunch with Roxanne when I announced my decision.

"I think I'm going to do it," I said.

Roxanne wrapped a paper towel around a frozen burrito and put it in the microwave. "Darling, I have no idea what you're talking about." She pushed several buttons, and the oven started.

"I'm letting Marc back in."

"You already did that, babycakes."

"In my bedroom."

I suddenly had her full attention. She sat down next to me. "Really."

"I'm ready to move on."

She smiled. "So things are going pretty well."

"More than well. Better than ever. Marc's been a complete saint. I think this whole thing was a giant wake-up call for him."

"Won't be the first time someone walked through hell to get to heaven," Roxanne said. The timer bell rang on the microwave, and Roxanne got up, opened the microwave door and reached inside and pulled out her burrito, lifting it by the corners of the paper towel. "So when are you doing this?"

"I was thinking of making him a nice dinner and telling him tonight. Do you think Jan could sit?"

"She's probably free and you know how she loves Char. Why don't you just have Charlotte sleep over? Just in case one thing leads to another."

✦

Jan was available, and I arranged for her to pick Charlotte up from school, then run by the house for pajamas and a change of clothes. The more I thought about the night, the more excited I got. I didn't call Marc to tell him—I wanted the evening to be a complete surprise. I left work at four, stopped at the grocery store and picked up a bottle of red wine, a loaf of peasant bread, asparagus and a couple of steaks. I put the steaks on to broil, then set the table with china, silverware and tall candlesticks.

Marc had told me that he would be home by 6:30, so at 6:20 I lit the candles, put on some perfume and waited for him in the front room. He didn't come. By 7:30 I began to worry that something had happened. By 8:30 my emotions started running wild and I began imagining him with the other woman. I called his office line, but it went straight to voicemail. I waited for him until eleven, then I blew out the candles, put the steaks in foil and went to bed without eating. My emotions vacillated from anger to worry. *Where was he?*

He didn't come home during the night. The next morning I called his work. His secretary, Gloria, put me through to Marc's boss, Dean.

"I was just about to call you," Dean said. "We were worried when Marc didn't show up today. Yesterday he was acting rather peculiar. He left work at noon to go to an appointment and missed an important meeting later in the day. No one has seen or heard from him since. We assumed he was at home."

"No, I haven't seen him since yesterday morning," I said. "What do you mean by peculiar?"

"He offered another salesman his two biggest accounts."

"Why would he do that?"

"It makes no sense," Dean said. "Gloria also said she overheard him on the phone earlier in the day. She thought he was . . . crying."

I thanked him and hung up. I was frightened. *Had I been too harsh?* That night, after Charlotte was in bed, Roxanne came over to the house and sat with me while I made calls to whoever I could think of who might have seen him. I called the area hospitals and police stations to see if he'd been in an accident. It was around nine when the headlights of Marc's car flashed through our picture window on our living room wall. Roxanne looked at me. "I'll go, babe. Good luck."

"Thanks."

Roxanne went out the side door to avoid bumping into him. I heard the door unlock, then Marc opened the front door and walked in. I walked into the foyer to meet him. He reeked of alcohol.

"Where have you been?"

"Gone," he said, avoiding eye contact.

"You've been drinking."

"Aren't you sharp."

"Marc, where have you been?"

"I don't have to answer to you."

"You're still my husband."

"Not for long."

"What's that supposed to mean?"

"I've been drinking," he said. "That's what it means. That's where I've been. That's all you need to know."

"You're on a real winning streak here. First cheating, now drinking."

He waved a clumsy hand to brush me off. "Don't talk to me. I'm through talking. I'm getting my things and leaving."

"You've been begging me to stay and now you're leaving?"

"Pretty much."

"What about Charlotte?"

"She's going to have to get used to it anyway."

"What are you talking about? Get used to what?"

"Being fatherless." He stopped to look me in the eyes. "Not that you care, but I found out why I'm not feeling well. I have pancreatic cancer. The doctor's given me two to six months to live. How do you like them apples?" He walked to our bedroom, knelt down at the dresser and began pulling out clothes.

I followed him, dumbstruck. When I could speak, I said, "Marc, I didn't even know you weren't feeling well."

"You weren't doing much thinking about how I was doing."

I crouched down next to him. "Marc, please stop. I do care. I was so afraid that something had happened to you. Thursday night I made us a candlelit dinner. I want you back."

He stopped what he was doing. "It's too late for that."

"No, it's not. Where will you go?"

He looked at me sadly. "If I'm lucky, I have maybe thirty to forty days left of any kind of quality. I'm not going to waste a single one of them being abused by you. I told you I'm sorry for what happened. But I'm done now. I'm not going to spend my last days on earth beating myself over what I can't change. Or let you do it." He stood, his arms full of clothing. "Where'd you put my suitcase?"

"Marc, what happened, the other woman, it broke my heart, because I love you. I've always loved you. And I forgive you for what happened."

He looked at me in disbelief.

"I forgive you, Marc. Completely. I want you back. I want things to be the way they were."

"They can't be the way they were."

"No, but there can still be love."

He took a deep breath. "I don't know."

"Where will you go?" My eyes welled up with tears. "Do you really want to die alone?"

His eyes began to moisten as well. He shook his head.

"You belong here with your family. We'll take care of you."

He laid his clothes on the bed, then wiped his eyes with his sleeve.

I took his hand. "I married you for better or for worse. Most of it has been better. You've been good to me. You've given me Charlotte. You're a good father. I want to be with you. I want you in my bed. It's forgotten. I promise."

"Can you really do that?"

I put my arms around him. "I will. I promise. Let me care for you."

He suddenly began to cry. "I'm so sorry about everything. I'm sorry I have this."

"We can beat this. *Together*, we can beat this."

He shook his head. "It's too late for that. My oncologist

said that even if they put me through chemo and radiation it would only buy me a few months at best. He said, 'Go home, put things in order and cherish every minute with your loved ones.' " He began to cry again. "I told him I didn't have a home."

"You do. You have us. And that's what we'll do. We'll make the most of every minute. I love you. I always have."

Marc dropped his head on my shoulder and we both wept.

CHAPTER

Eight

Just when I was ready to take the bandage off my nose,
an axe took off my head.

✦ Beth Cardall's Diary ✦

Physically, Marc did okay for the next three weeks, but it was clear that the cancer was spreading. Almost as difficult as watching his decline was watching Charlotte experience his loss. Telling her that her father was dying was the most difficult thing I'd ever done. It was hard to know how much she really perceived. What does a six-year-old know of death? For that matter, what does anyone really know?

By August, Marc had difficulty walking and I took a leave of absence from work to care for him. On a cool morning in September, I had just finished bathing him when he asked, "Do you love me?"

"Of course I do," I said, drawing a terry cloth towel across his back. "Haven't I shown you?"

"In spades," he said quietly.

"Why do you ask?"

"I wonder if you would love the *real* me."

"What do you mean?"

"Never mind," he said.

I pushed the exchange from my mind, chalking it up to the myriad drugs the doctors had him on. About a week later I was feeding him lunch when he mumbled, *"E pluribus unum."*

E pluribus unum?

"I need to confess something."

The way he said this filled my chest with fear. I instinctively knew that whatever he was going to say was bad. "I don't want to hear it," I said. "If it's going to hurt me, please don't tell me."

"I don't want to die a liar. I don't want our relationship to have just been a lie."

My panic was now so thick I could barely breathe. "Please, Marc, don't do this."

He said, "Ashley wasn't the only one. There were others."

Others? I looked at him waiting for the other shoe to drop. When he didn't say it, I asked, "How many?"

"Maybe eleven."

Eleven. I began to cry. My heart wasn't a yo-yo; it was a paper target on a shooting range. It was roadkill. "You couldn't have just kept this to yourself?" I got up and walked out of the room.

Nothing was the same after that. Marc was a stranger to me—a man I'd never really known. I didn't speak to him for the next three days. Oddly, I wasn't angry—emotionally, that account had been bankrupted—I was something more. I was indifferent.

Marc stayed in our bedroom while I slept with Charlotte in her bed. I don't think it was coincidence that his confession was the start of his great decline. He lived for just three and a half weeks more and I cared for him through it all. It wasn't easy. I'm neither a doormat nor a saint. I stayed with him because of Charlotte. She was still sick, complaining every few days of a stomachache, no doubt made worse by her fear and anxiety over what was happening to her dad. I wasn't about to punish her for the sins of her father. Besides, Marc had nowhere else to go, and regardless of how much I'd been hurt, I couldn't live with my daughter's father dying alone, even though more than once I wished I could have.

On the third day of October the hospice workers started their vigil. My husband, they told me, was actively dying (which sounded to me like an oxymoron). I had no doubt that Marc was sorry for what he'd done, sorry for his betrayal, even more sorry, I think, that he had told me. Those were his last words to me, the saddest last words one could leave this world with: "I'm sorry."

A week later, on October 10, he passed quietly in the night. Charlotte cried for her father the entire next day and every day after for the next two weeks. By then my heart already felt like it had died a hundred times over.

Marc had a small life insurance policy, only $25,000, which wasn't enough to do much more than cover his medical deductibles and funeral expenses and to catch up on the bills that had piled up since we had both stopped working.

That is where Charlotte and I were as the year came to a close. Winter came again and the days shortened and seemed darker and colder than ever before.

Then the holiday season crept upon us. I did not welcome it. I was feeling anything but festive, anything but believing.

I was trustless of life and men. I would say that I was without faith, but no one is truly faithless; they just have faith in the wrong things: fear and defeat.

Then, when I least expected anything new in my life, he came.

CHAPTER

Nine

*I have found that the most significant experiences
of our lives rarely come when we're expecting them
and oftentimes when we're not even paying attention.*

✦ Beth Cardall's Diary ✦

The first time I saw *him* was on Christmas Day, 1989. As the Bing Crosby song had it, it was a white Christmas. Actually, more of a *white-out* Christmas. Nearly thirty inches of heavy snow had fallen during the night, and it was still falling, with brisk winds sculpting the snow along the roadsides into four-foot-high curled drifts that looked like frozen ocean waves. The radio said that more than five thousand homes in the city had lost electricity. Charlotte and I were among the fortunate who still had power and a cozy fire in our wood-burning stove.

Our Christmas tree looked like I felt inside: small, sparse and dry, with too few lights. Truthfully, I felt ugly, inside and out. I had been pretty once, or at least that seemed to be the general consensus, but not so much lately. I felt worn-out and broken, like an old running shoe. *Through the ringer*, my mother used to say. It sounds silly to me now, but I was only twenty-eight and I already felt old. I was much too young to feel that old.

Had I been alone I probably would have just ignored the season, but Charlotte really needed the holiday and Roxanne wouldn't have let me off that easy. We celebrated Thanksgiving Day with Roxanne and her family. The next Saturday, in a quest to capture the spirit, Charlotte and I made Christmas tree ornaments. We dipped walnuts in Elmer's glue and glitter and tied them with yarn. We also cut snowflakes from paper.

Money was tight, but I stretched to get Charlotte what she wanted, a Skip-It, a set of *Baby-sitters Club* books and her big present, an American Girl doll. She squealed when she opened the package with the doll.

"Look, Mom, what Santa brought!"

"She's beautiful. What's her name?"

"Molly."

"She wears glasses."

"Uh-huh. Like me. And a locket." She opened the doll's tiny locket around its neck. "Can we put a picture inside?"

I smiled. "How did you know to put a picture in there?"

"Everyone knows that."

"Sorry. Should we put a picture of you in there?"

"No, Daddy's."

She had been playing with her doll for a half-hour or so when she asked, "Mom, why didn't Santa bring you anything?"

"Well," I said, "I really didn't need anything so I asked Santa to give my presents to a good little girl who did."

"Doesn't Santa have enough for everyone?"

When did she get so smart? "Not this year. I guess there was a toy shortage at the North Pole."

I could see her puzzling over the dilemma. After a moment she said, "Then I'll ask Jesus to bring you something."

I smiled. "What are you going to ask Him to bring me?"

"Someone to take care of you."

Out of the mouths of babes, they say. I didn't know how to respond to that so I just changed the subject. "Are you hungry?"

She nodded. "Are we going to have muffins?"

"Yes we are. Just like I promised."

A week earlier I had asked Charlotte what she wanted for Christmas breakfast. She didn't hesitate: blueberry-buttermilk muffins. Blueberry-buttermilk muffins were our own creation. One Sunday morning I'd been in the middle of making muffins when I discovered we were out of milk. I didn't have time to run to the store so I substituted buttermilk. The results were unexpectedly delicious and a new favorite.

I went into the kitchen and began putting the ingredients together when I realized I'd forgotten the buttermilk. I could have just used regular milk or even just poured her some Cheerios—with the weather being the way it was, that would have been the prudent thing to do—but after what she'd been through that year, I didn't want to deny her anything that was within my grasp to deliver.

"We need to go to the store," I said. I put on my overcoat, bundled up Charlotte, then drove to the only place open Christmas morning—a 7-Eleven about a mile from my home.

Maybe it was chance, or perhaps it was in answer to Charlotte's prayer, but that's where I first saw *him*.

When we arrived at the 7-Eleven, I said to Charlotte, "Honey, just wait in the car. I'm only going to be a minute."

"Can I have some gum?"

I smiled. "Sure."

I was stomping the snow from my boots as I entered the store, so I didn't see him at first. He was standing near the back sipping coffee from a foam cup, staring at me intently.

We had brief eye contact. I tried not to stare, but he really was gorgeous. *Soap opera gorgeous*, Roxanne would say. Gorgeous and exotic looking. He had slightly curly, cappuccino-hued hair and bright blue eyes, which were radiant against his olive skin. I wondered what such a beautiful man was doing alone at a 7-Eleven on Christmas morning. Call it sour grapes, but the self-preservation part of my mind kicked in and I immediately concluded that there must be something wrong with him—like the time Charlotte made Kool-Aid and used salt instead of sugar. It looked good, but after one sip I poured the pitcher down the sink.

I stopped to pick up a few things besides my buttermilk—an apple, a half-gallon of milk and a package of Doublemint gum—then I walked to the cash register, my purchases balanced precariously in my arms.

He walked up to the counter at the same time, his eyes never leaving me. His gaze made me feel awkward, but, frankly, it was nice to be noticed.

"Merry Christmas," he said. His voice was warm and rich.

I had pretended that I hadn't noticed him staring at me and I turned and flashed a furtive smile. "Good morning," I said, then turned back to the clerk, doing my best to look uninterested.

As I was setting my things on the counter, the gum fell to the ground. I bent over to get it. Apparently *soap opera guy* had the same idea and we bumped heads hard. I stood up rubbing the top of my head. "Ow."

"I'm sorry," he said, grimacing with embarrassment. He handed me the package of Doublemint. "I'm Matthew."

I took the gum, still rubbing my head with the other hand. "Hi, Matthew."

"Have we met?"

I shook my head, wondering if this was a pickup line. "I don't think so."

The store clerk, who seemed oblivious to everything but his wish to be elsewhere, said, "Is this everything?"

"And this," I said. I handed him the gum, then fished a ten-dollar bill from my wallet.

"Six seventy-three out of ten." He handed me my change. "Would you like your things in a sack?"

"Yes, please."

I glanced back at Matthew and he smiled at me. I nervously brushed the hair back from my face. The clerk stacked everything in the sack and handed it to me. "Merry Christmas," he said dully.

I took the sack. "Thank you. You too."

I had turned to go when Matthew asked, "Do you work at a dry cleaner?"

I looked back at him. "Yes."

"Over on Highland Drive," he said. "I've seen you there."

I wondered how that was possible. I knew that I had never seen him. I definitely would have remembered, especially since Roxanne would have done something embarrassing like telling him I was single or taken his picture. "Then I'm sure I'll see you around," I said. "Merry Christmas." I walked back outside, where the snow had already begun to cover my windshield, and climbed into my car.

"Here's your gum, Char."

"Thanks, Mommy."

I looked at myself in the rear-view mirror. No makeup, and my hair was a mess pulled back with a scarf. *Why would someone that gorgeous be hitting on me?*

CHAPTER

Ten

You might think that those who would most look forward to the new year are those eager to leave the past behind— but it's not usually so. If you hated your last dentist appointment, you don't look forward to the next.

✴ Beth Cardall's Diary ✴

The holidays are a cyclical time for dry cleaners. Prompt was always crazy busy up until Thanksgiving, slow until Christmas then *pedal to the metal* the week before New Year's as people cleaned out their closets and got ready for their New Year's Eve festivities.

Prompt Cleaners closed early on New Year's Eve, at 2 P.M., so we were slammed all morning with people picking up their formal wear for New Year's Eve parties. I was pressing pants when Roxanne came back. "What's cookin', Beth?"

"Besides me?" I asked through a blast of steam. It was always ten degrees warmer in back next to the big machinery, the massive dry-cleaning machines that could swallow thirty-five pounds of dinner jackets in one sitting.

"Here's your check," she said, handing me an envelope. "Don't spend it all in one place."

"I'm afraid I already did," I said.

Roxanne leaned back against the shirt press. "Can you believe it's the last day of the decade?"

"Good riddance," I replied.

She grinned at my response. "My, aren't you little Miss Sunshine. Does sourpuss have any hot New Year's Eve plans?"

"I'm making cheese enchiladas for Charlotte. That's about as hot as it will get. What about you?"

"Ray's working, so it's just Jan and me. I'm making my chocolate fondue. Why don't you and Char come over with your enchiladas and watch Dick Clark with us?"

"Thanks, but Charlotte wasn't doing all that well this morning. We'll probably just go to bed early."

"Oh, you're a barrel of fun. You're not at all excited for the new decade?"

"I'm broke, alone, and working in a sweatshop. What do you think?"

"I *think* you need someone."

I looked up at her. "I have Charlotte."

"A *male* companion."

"You sound like Charlotte. She prayed that Jesus would bring me someone. I don't think Jesus runs a dating service."

"I wouldn't be too sure of that. Wouldn't it be nice to have someone to take care of you?"

"Yes, that's a lovely fiction. Unfortunately, not everyone can be Ray."

"You don't think Ray has problems?"

"Everyone has problems. But you don't have to marry them."

"You don't really want to just sit around alone on New Year's Eve. That's . . ."

"Pathetic?" I said.

"I was going for boring, but pathetic works."

I kept pressing. "I'll think about it."

Roxanne folded her arms. "You're not coming over, are you, party-pooper?"

"Look, Rox, I'm not in the mood to celebrate. You know what I've been through."

"Then don't think of it as a celebration. Think of it as a wake for a bad year."

"Thanks for the invite."

She sighed. "All right. I gotta get back up front. Enjoy your enchiladas, killjoy."

Roxanne and I locked the front doors at the two o'clock closing but still got the frantic last-minute crush of people who had forgotten their evening wear and pounded on the front and back doors begging for us to open. It was nearly three when Roxanne and I finally snuck out the back.

"Offer's still good," Roxanne said, unlocking her car. "Chocolate fondue and strawberries and bananas for dipping."

"We'll see."

"That's what you tell your children when you don't want to say no, but mean to."

"Love you, Rox," I said. "Happy New Year."

"You too, baby. Let's hope for a better one."

I drove across the street to the bank to deposit my check, then over to the grocery store to pick up a few things for our 'celebration'—a six-pack of root beer, a package of cinnamon bears, a can of tomato sauce, some cheddar cheese and corn tortillas.

As I waited in the checkout line, *soap opera guy*, the man I met Christmas Day at the 7-Eleven, stepped in line after me. He was just as beautiful as I remembered.

"Déjà vu," he said.

I looked at him, trying to remember his name. "Mike," I guessed.

He grinned, a slight dimple appearing above his right cheek. "Matthew."

"Right, Matthew. The head-butter."

He chuckled. "I like that, Matthew, the head-butter. I'm still embarrassed about that."

Without acknowledging me, the woman cashier started scanning my items and dropping them in a plastic sack.

"So what do you do for an encore," I asked, "a body slam?"

He laughed. "Yeah, well, if they hung me for being grace-ful, I'd die innocent."

The cashier said, "That will be eight dollars and seventy-four cents."

"I should have that," I said. I dug into my purse, hoping that I had enough cash to not write a check. All I could find was six dollars.

"Here," Matthew said, handing the cashier a ten-dollar bill.

I looked up at him. "I got it," I said. I rooted back through my purse in vain. Finally, I brought out my checkbook and started writing. "Eight dollars and . . . seventy-two cents?"

"Seventy-four," the woman said curtly, doing her best to look annoyed that I was writing a check for such a small amount. I finished scribbling the amount and handed her the check.

"I need I.D.," the clerk said.

"Really? For eight dollars?" Matthew asked.

"I don't make the rules," she said.

"I'll get it," I said. I got back in my purse, brought out my wallet and showed her my driver's license.

She stamped the back of the check, wrote down my driver's license number and put the check in the till.

I looked back at Matthew a little embarrassed. "Bye."

"Hey, would you hold on a second?"

I looked at him quizzically. "Why?"

"I just want to talk to you. I'll just be a second. I promise. Please."

I'm not sure why I said yes—maybe something as simple and powerful as social pressure—but I relented. "Okay. Just for a few minutes. I really need to get home."

"That's all I need," he said.

I walked over near the automatic doors to wait for him. He handed the clerk a couple bills and said, "Keep the change." He walked up to me smiling. "Thanks for waiting. Got a big party tonight?"

"Oh, yeah. We'll be swinging from the chandeliers."

"Sounds fun," he said, as if he believed me.

"So, are you stalking me?"

His smile broadened. "You're a direct woman, so I'll just cut to the chase and ask you out."

"You want to ask me out?"

"I do."

"What if I told you that I'm not interested?"

"I'd expect that."

"But would it deter you?"

"Probably not. It's a new year. I'm betting you could use a friend."

"I have enough friends. Besides, men never just want to be friends."

"Maybe I'm the exception."

"*That* would worry me." I looked at him, feeling a little sympathetic for his situation. "Look, you seem like a nice guy and I'm sure you know you're very handsome, but I'm not looking for a new relationship in my life right now. I'm flattered, really. But I'm not interested. Sorry."

He stood there looking at me, completely unfazed by what I thought was a pretty clear dismissal. "You're honest. I like that."

"Which only shows that you haven't been around me long enough. No one wants that much honesty."

"You're right, it would probably drive me crazy. When can I take you out?"

I looked at him in astonishment. "You didn't hear a word I said, did you?"

"I'm a poor listener."

"Listen . . ."

"Matthew," he said.

"Right. Matthew, you know nothing about me. You don't

even know my name. So let's leave it at that. Trust me, that would be best." I turned to leave.

"It's Bethany," he said.

I turned back. "What?"

"Your name is Bethany."

"How did you know that?"

He shrugged. "I must have heard someone call you that."

"No one calls me Bethany except my mother. And she passed away ten years ago."

He just looked at me. "Then it's a mystery."

I said, "I really need to go."

"Wait, please. I just want to ask you out. I won't take no for an answer."

"Take it or not, that's still the answer." I walked away. He followed me out to the parking lot.

When I was unlocking my car, he said, "Why won't you give me a chance?"

I opened my car door. "I told you why. Besides, now you've set off all my internal warning bells. Bye."

"I'm not giving up," he said.

"Bye." I climbed inside my car.

I started my car and backed out. He stood there, his hands in his pockets, watching me. *What did he want?* Roxanne would have smacked me over the top of the head for turning him down.

CHAPTER

Eleven

"Alas, another year."

✦ Beth Cardall's Diary ✦

New Year's Eve was even quieter than usual—which, for me, is saying something. Marc and I had never really been big on New Year's celebrations. For the first few years of our marriage we went to his company's New Year's Eve party, until one year Marc's boss, Dean, had had too much to drink and hit on me while Marc was talking to one of the other salesmen. He told me the only reason he'd hired Marc was to get to me. I was mortified. "It's never happening," I said, "and if you ever tell my husband that, I'm telling your wife." I went and found Marc and asked him to take me home.

After that we never went to the company party again. I never told Marc about what had happened, I feared it would have broken his all-too-fragile ego. I just told him that I didn't want to go again. He acted angry with me but didn't put up much of a fight.

Since then, New Year's had become consequential only in that I bought a new calendar and we could sleep in the next morning.

Charlotte had spent the day playing at the home of a neighbor, her best friend Katie. Katie's mother, Margaret Wirthlin, was a sweet, matronly woman with eight children.

She was always happy to have Charlotte around, and frankly, with that many children, I don't think she even noticed an extra one.

I picked up Charlotte on the way home from work. Again, she wasn't feeling well. Once we were home she just lay on the couch as I made the enchiladas and fell asleep before I finished. I considered just letting her sleep, but I was so worried about her losing weight that I woke her for dinner. She took only two bites of her enchilada, then laid her head on the table. I carried her to my bed, where she had slept since Marc's passing.

I went back out to the kitchen and did the dishes, then lay down on the couch to read a book.

This was it, the utter excitement of my life. As I thought of the new year, my heart was filled with dread. I don't know when I had ever felt so vulnerable or hopeless. It seemed that I was assailed on every side. I was lonely, physically and mentally exhausted, spiritually numb, and financially I was walking a shaky tightrope that a small, well-timed breeze could knock me off of. My salary wasn't enough to pay the mortgage and our expenses. Without Marc's income, I knew that I needed to get a job that paid more, but doing what? I had no "marketable" skills, no résumé, and with all the missed days because of Charlotte's health, who would keep me?

In spite of my fears, in the back of my mind I harbored a far greater one—one I pushed down to the deepest recesses of my mind. *What if Charlotte was fighting something bigger than anyone had guessed?* She wasn't getting worse, at least she didn't seem to be, but she also wasn't getting any better. What if it was something chronic? *What if it was something terminal?* I immediately pushed the thought from my mind. I couldn't take that. *Anything but that.*

It would be nice, as both Charlotte and Roxanne had wished for me, to have someone to take care of me. But I might as well be wishing for a fairy godmother. It wasn't going to happen. I had built walls around my life and heart not because I liked the solitude, I didn't; I built them to protect Charlotte and me. In spite of my claims to the contrary, I am one of those women who hates being alone. Even after the betrayals I had suffered by Marc, I still missed him. At least I thought I did, until it occurred to me that I didn't miss *him,* I missed the *delusion of him*—the delusion of our love and family. Like everyone else, I wanted to be loved. I wanted to belong to someone. I wanted to be wanted. But at what cost? I feared that my emotional state was as precarious as my financial one—just one misstep away from disaster.

My eyes filled with tears. When had life gotten so mean? Better question, when hadn't it been? I'd been alone since I was eighteen, when my mother passed away during a routine gallbladder operation. My aunt stepped in for a while, but it was obvious to me that it was out of obligation, not desire. At eighteen you're pretty much on your own anyway. I met Marc my sophomore year in college and jumped when he popped the question. I'm not saying I didn't love him. I just didn't love him as much as I hated being alone. And I paid for it.

Was there someone else out there for me? My thoughts drifted to the man at the store. Matthew. Was I pushing away exactly what I was hoping for? Would it have killed me to let him in, just a little? To put my toe in the water? He seemed sincere. He seemed nice enough.

Nice. I grimaced at the thought. *Another nice guy. Like Marc.* Maybe it's the nice guys who aren't to be trusted. Maybe it was the very façade of "nice" one should avoid; sheep's clothing, right? *Better the devil we know.*

The bottom line was, I didn't know. I didn't know whom, if anyone, I could trust. The only thing I knew for certain was whom I couldn't trust: me. Or at least my sense of discernment. For seven years I had lived a charade. For seven years my husband, my best friend, my soul mate, had moved through a succession of women while I minded the home fires oblivious to it all. What a fool I was. I mean, really, how stupid could a woman be?

I suppose that all I knew for certain was that I couldn't be drained again. There was too little left—my heart too close to empty.

At midnight I could hear the pop of firecrackers and Roman candles from across the street and the ruckus of Margaret's clan beating pans together in their front yard. I looked out the window. "Happy New Year," I said to no one. And I said it without hope. Happiness was a dark horse.

CHAPTER

Twelve

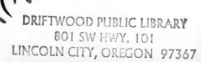

This man just keeps coming back like a flesh-covered boomerang. I hope he's not crooked too.

✦ Beth Cardall's Diary ✦

I was glad for the holidays to be over and for things to get back to normal, whatever that was these days. I was pressing suit coats when Teresa minced her way back to my station. Teresa was Prompt's token bombshell, a stunningly beautiful nineteen-year-old blonde—former homecoming queen, head cheerleader, you know the type. Roxanne opined that Teresa's main purpose for existence was to remind her of how old and undesirable she'd become.

Teresa had pulled her Walkman's earphones down around her neck, and her face was bent in a wide smile. "Beth, someone sent you flowers."

I looked up from the press. "Me?" I couldn't guess who would be sending me flowers.

"Yes, you. They're beautiful. And, by the way, you can keep the flowers, I'll keep the deliveryman. He's hot. I told him he could just leave the flowers with me, but he said he needed to deliver them personally."

The dry cleaner had a two-way mirror behind the front counter so that when we were shorthanded we could work in back and keep an eye on the lobby. I looked around my rack of coats to see this deliveryman she was talking about.

Matthew was standing at the counter holding a vase of sunflowers. I went back to the suit coat I was working on, lightly sighing. "I'll be there in a minute."

Teresa looked at me in astonishment. "Aren't you dying to find out who sent them?"

"I know who sent them. They're from the man holding them."

She looked at me incredulously. "You've got to be kidding."

"What do you mean by that?"

"Nothing," she said quickly. "Nothing. So, are you coming or should I send the Disney Prince away?"

I hung the coat I was pressing on the rack. "I'll be right there."

"Then I'll give you some space. Have fun." Teresa ran off to the bathroom. I looked back through the glass. Matthew stood patiently, swaying a little to the lobby's music, the large blue vase clasped in his hands. I shook my head then walked out to the front. He smiled as I came through the door. "Hi, Beth."

"Hi." I put my hands on my hips. "I told you—"

"I brought you these," he said, thrusting the flowers toward me. "I told you I wasn't going to give up."

For a moment I just looked at them, unsure of what to do. Taking them was counter to what I had convinced myself was right, but when you've been on a diet sometimes you just have to have a little chocolate, if you know what I mean. *Besides*, I rationalized, *what kind of woman rejects a man offering her flowers?*

"Thank you," I said, taking the bouquet and setting it on the counter. "I love sunflowers."

"I know."

"How would you know that?"

"You just seem like the kind of woman who would. Roses are pretty but sunflowers have meaning."

I looked at him quizzically. That was something I had often said to Charlotte. *Sunflowers look to the sun,* I told her. *They mean hope.*

"What do sunflowers mean?" I asked.

He looked at me and a knowing smile crossed his lips. "Hope."

As I looked at him, I couldn't help but think how handsome he was. My eyes moved back and forth between him and the equally beautiful bouquet of flowers. Finally, I sighed. "What do you want?"

"Just one date. If you hate it, or me, I promise I'll leave you alone."

"Okay," I said.

His eyebrows rose with surprise. "Really?"

"Well you're not going to give up until I go out with you, are you?"

"No."

"Then what choice do I have? One date. When?"

"When's good for you?"

"My babysitter is usually only available on weekends."

"How about Friday?" he asked.

"This Friday?"

He nodded. "Yes."

"Babysitter willing, Friday it is. What time?"

"Seven P.M.?"

"Friday, seven P.M. I'll plan on it."

He smiled broadly. "Great." He started to leave, then turned back. "I don't know your address."

I pulled a sheet of paper from the order pad by the register and scribbled my address on the back. "It's the home with the blue door." I handed it to him and he looked at it, then folded it up and shoved it in his pocket.

"See you then."

I watched him leave, then I carried my flowers to the back. I was such a sucker for flowers. Always had been. Still, I couldn't help but wonder if I had done the right thing.

Roxanne was standing next to the press waiting for me. Teresa had alerted her to my caller, and the two of them had watched the exchange from behind the mirror. "Now I know why you didn't want to come over on New Year's."

"What are you talking about?" I set the flowers down on the counter behind the press.

"You've been holding out on me, girl. I've been telling you to get back on the horse and you've been bronco busting all along."

"Bronco busting?"

"I saw that man. Why didn't you tell me about him?"

"There was nothing to tell."

"Nothing to tell? How long has it been going on?"

"We just met." I went back to work, putting a coat on the press.

"Where?"

"At a 7-Eleven."

"Wow, all I ever get there is Diet Coke. Who made the first move?"

"Who do you think?"

"What did he say?"

"If you must know—"

"I must," she inserted.

"He head-butted me."

"What?"

"It was an accident. I dropped my gum."

"I don't care. A man that fine can head-butt me up Main and down State. So why aren't you acting thrilled about this?"

"Because *I'm not* thrilled about this. It doesn't feel right."

"Because of Marc?"

"Yes, but it's more than that. I mean, look at this guy."

"Yeah, I saw him. He's gorgeous. What's the problem?"

"Have you ever been sitting in the stands at a ball game and someone turns around and waves at you and you smile and start to wave back when you realize they're waving to someone behind you?"

"Yeah."

"That's how I feel."

Roxanne rested her hands on her hips. "Well, girl, look at those flowers. He's definitely waving at you."

"It just doesn't feel right. He's younger, painfully handsome, and nice."

"What a nightmare . . ."

"Come on, Rox, you have to admit that it doesn't make sense."

"No, you need to admit that it *does*. Why can't you just accept that someone might find you desirable?"

I frowned. "I don't know. Probably because I feel like damaged goods." I went back to pressing. "Besides, my heart tells me not to trust it. It's the first rule of love and money—if it sounds too good to be true, it is."

"You're too cynical."

"I'm just trying to be smart for a change."

"If running from happiness is smart, then I'd rather be dumb. Better dumb than lonely."

"Well, I'm both."

"Just give it a try, Beth. You've had a rough year. Have a little fun for a change. What's the worst thing that could happen?"

I looked up at her. "I could like him."

CHAPTER

Thirteen

We rarely worry about the correct things.

✦ Beth Cardall's Diary ✦

Friday morning Matthew came by the cleaners. Roxanne was up front when he came in.

"Is Beth here?"

"She sure is," she said. "You're Matthew?"

"Yes, ma'am."

"My mother is ma'am. I'm Rox. I'll get her for you." She ran back to get me, her face bright with excitement. "He's here."

"Who's here?"

"*Him.* Matthew."

"Oh." I looked up through the glass. He was standing there, his hands in his pockets. I hung up the trousers and walked up front.

He smiled when he saw me. "Good morning."

"Hi."

"I was just making sure we're still on for tonight."

I nodded. "I found a babysitter."

He smiled. "Awesome. Then I'll see you at seven."

"Seven it is."

"Do you like Italian food?"

"I love Italian."

"Great. I was thinking dinner and a movie." He just stood there awkwardly, then said again, "Well, great. See you at seven." He turned and walked out.

Roxanne walked in before the front door closed. "Girl, that boy is smitten."

"Will you quit spying on me?"

"No way."

I shook my head and walked back to the press. Roxanne followed me back.

"So what are you and the hunk doing on your date?"

"Dinner and a show."

"No show—bad choice for a first date. Movies are for old, boring couples who have run out of things to say. Like me and Ray."

"It's not my choice."

"You're the woman, it's always your choice. Just take your time at dinner and then suggest something else. Trust me, smitten as he is, he's eager to please."

"Suggest something else, like what?"

"Girl, you're almost thirty. Think of something."

I shook my head. "No. Absolutely not. Nothing physical. Not even a kiss."

"Are you really trying to run him off?"

"Maybe. Besides, he said he just wants to be friends."

She looked at me incredulously. "He didn't say that."

"Yes, he did."

"He *really* said that?"

"Yes," I repeated. "He *really* said that."

"When?"

"At the supermarket."

"Then he's a liar. Men never want to just be friends. And if he does, then you should really worry."

"That's what I told him."

"Good, you're not completely numb." She touched my hair. "When was the last time you got a cut?"

"Five weeks ago."

"It'll pass. So here's what you do. After dinner, get a coffee to go, drive up Millcreek Canyon and just sit in the car and talk."

"Why don't we just get a coffee at the restaurant?"

"This isn't about food, it's about strategic placement."

I held up my hands. "Stop right there. This isn't about strategic anything. I have no place in my life for complications. If he can carry a conversation, we're fine. If not, then lucky me, I dodged a bullet."

Roxanne sighed. "Okay, fine. You're right. Boring as all get out, but right. What time is he coming over?"

"Seven."

"Jan will be over at 6:45. And I expect a full report in the morning."

"That I can do. Now let me work, boss."

"Okay, okay." As she walked back out front, she shouted after me, "Remember, *full* report."

I smiled. *I love that woman.*

Jan arrived around six-thirty. I had just gotten out of the shower when Charlotte let her in. I came out wrapped in a towel.

"Hi, Mrs. C." Jan was dressed in a maroon baby-doll dress with black tights and a denim jacket.

"I'm sorry," I said. "I thought I said seven."

"You did," Jan said brightly, "I'm off the clock until seven. You know, I just love hanging with my Char."

"Thanks, honey. I made Charlotte some Ramen noodles for dinner. I'll be in the bathroom getting ready."

I went back and got dressed then started on my makeup. It had been a while since I'd put that much time in at the mirror and it made me happy. It felt good to feel pretty again. I was putting on my mascara when I heard Jan scream, "Mrs. Cardall! Mrs. Cardall!"

I dropped my mascara and ran out to the kitchen. Charlotte was lying on the kitchen floor shaking. Her eyelids were fluttering and her body stiffening. Jan was kneeling beside her, pale as milk. I dropped to Charlotte's side. "She's having a seizure. Call 911!"

Jan popped up and ran to the phone while I held Charlotte's shoulders. "Honey, it's Mom."

"It's 911," Jan said. "What's your address?"

"Twenty-four twelve Oakhurst," I said, "tell them to hurry!"

Jan repeated the address. "They want to know what's happening."

"She's having a seizure."

"They want to know if she's had one before?"

"No. What do I do?" I said, trying to stay calm.

"What do we do?" Jan turned back. "Roll her to her side."

Charlotte suddenly went limp. "Charlotte!" I screamed to Jan, "Tell them she passed out. Do I need to hold her tongue?"

She repeated my words into the phone. "Is she still breathing?"

"Yes."

"Don't put anything in her mouth. They say she'll be all right. Put something soft under her head."

I took off my sweater, rolled it up and put it under her head. A moment later Charlotte moaned, then began to move. I said to her softly, "Honey, can you hear me?"

She looked up at me and began to cry.

I cupped Charlotte's face. "I'm here, sweetheart. I'm here." I heard the wail of a siren coming down our street.

CHAPTER

Fourteen

Fear thrives best in the shadow of the unknown.

✦ Beth Cardall's Diary ✦

It was shortly after 10 P.M., and I was sitting next to Charlotte in her hospital bed when Roxanne arrived. Charlotte had been calm and sleeping for nearly an hour. Roxanne put her hand on my shoulder as she looked at Charlotte. "Praise God," she said softly. She hugged me, then we stepped out of the room to talk.

"What was it?" Roxanne asked.

"She had a grand mal seizure."

"Do they know what caused it?"

"No. By the time she got to the hospital, she was fine. You'd almost think nothing had happened."

"Is it related to the other stuff she's been going through?"

"I don't know. Maybe. But whatever it is, it's getting worse." Tears began to well up in my eyes. "I'm just so afraid. What if I lose her too?"

"Don't even go there. You're not going to lose her."

"I wish you could promise me that."

I started to cry and fell into Roxanne. She gently rubbed my back. "It's okay, baby. It's okay."

A few minutes later, when I could speak, I asked, "How's Jan?"

"She's a little shaken up, but she'll be okay. She's never been through anything like that before."

"Did she tell you what happened?"

"She said Char was just eating when she started talking funny. She asked her if she was being silly, and she said Charlotte just looked at her then started shaking."

I groaned. "Thank goodness she was there. I was in the bathroom getting ready when it happened, I wouldn't have even known." I choked up again.

Roxanne put her arm around me. "She's okay, that's what matters." After a few minutes she asked, "How did your date react to all the excitement?"

"My date," I said. I had completely forgotten about Matthew. "It happened before he got there. I don't even have his phone number. He probably just thinks I stood him up."

"Well, don't worry about it. If he's a keeper, he'll understand. And if he doesn't, you don't need him."

"I don't need him anyway," I said. "I don't need anyone new in my life right now. If tonight taught me anything, it's that Charlotte needs me. She's already lost one parent—I can't divide my time any more than it already is. She needs all of me."

"Okay, okay," Roxanne said, calming me. "I understand."

Just then a doctor walked into the room. "Mrs. Cardall?" he said, looking between Roxanne and me.

"I'm Mrs. Cardall."

"I'm Dr. Hansen. Could I speak to you for a moment?"

"Of course."

The doctor looked at Roxanne. "Alone."

"It's okay," I said. "She's family."

He nodded. "I just want to update you on where we stand. Clearly, she's had a seizure, but we don't think it's related to her other health problems. I've gone back and reviewed her records, and I want to do a few more tests to see if we can't narrow things down a bit more. I'm particularly concerned about all of the abdominal pain she's been experiencing."

I was tired of hearing this. "Don't you even have a guess what it could be?"

"They're just guesses, but I want to test for Crohn's disease and Whipple's disease."

My heart froze. "Are either of them terminal?"

"Please, I'm not saying that she has either of those diseases. Some of the symptoms are there, but it's way too early to tell. Whipple's disease is a rare bacterial infection that affects the gastrointestinal system. Now, it can be serious without proper treatment, and if diagnosed too late it can cause irreversible damage to the central nervous system, but it has been successfully treated with antibiotics, typically over the course of one or two years."

I started crying. Roxanne put her arm around me.

"What is Crohn's?" Roxanne asked.

"It's a bowel disease that causes inflammation of the lining of the digestive tract. That would explain the abdominal pain she's been having."

"Is it . . ." Roxanne looked at me and stopped.

"Terminal? No. Crohn's is painful and can lead to more serious ailments, but therapies can bring about relief and even long-term remission."

Neither sounded good. *How much more did she have to suffer?* I thought. "When will you do the tests?" I asked.

"We'd like to do some of them now," he said, "while she's still in the hospital."

"We need to know what's wrong. I can't take this any-more."

"To diagnose Whipple's we generally have to perform an upper endoscopy, and for Crohn's a colonoscopy. We would like to recommend you to a gastroenterologist who will fa-miliarize you with these procedures."

"Is it expensive?" I asked.

"It should be covered by your insurance."

After Marc died, his work had put me on their COBRA plan, but I couldn't afford the monthly premium and in Janu-ary I let it lapse. "We don't have health insurance anymore," I said.

Roxanne put her hand on my back. "Ray and I can help."

"You can't do that," I said. "I'll get a loan."

The doctor looked at me sympathetically. "Let's do this: We'll first run another blood test to see if her anemia has improved. If it's better, we might be able to rule out an upper endoscopy. We'll put off the colonoscopy until we're sure it's not Whipple's."

"Thank you," I said.

"You're welcome," Dr. Hansen said. "Have a good night." He walked off.

"I can't stand this," I said to Roxanne. I put my head on her shoulder and cried.

CHAPTER

Fifteen

*It is not good fences that make good neighbors.
It is good hearts.*

✦ Beth Cardall's Diary ✦

The next day the hospital staff ran another blood test. Despite the iron supplements Charlotte had been taking for the last few weeks, her anemia had not improved, indicative of both Whipple's and Crohn's. I had to remind myself that these were still just guesses. I made an appointment with the pediatric gastroenterologist Dr. Hansen had recommended. His soonest opening was two weeks away.

Early Sunday morning I brought Charlotte home from the hospital. Between the nurses' frequent visits and my worry for Charlotte, I had slept very little the night before, and I went right to bed. A little before noon our doorbell rang. It was my neighbor, Margaret, her daughter Katie, and one of her six sons. They came bearing gifts: a chicken broccoli casserole, a loaf of homemade wheat bread and an apple crisp. Katie brought a Get-well card she had made for Charlotte.

"You didn't need to do this," I said.

"Nonsense, that's what neighbors are for. We just love your Charlotte. She's such a dear little girl." Margaret raised the glass dish she was carrying. "Can we bring these in for you?"

"Of course. Thank you."

Margaret and her son carried the food inside and set everything on the counter. Charlotte was on the sofa playing with Molly and lit up when she saw Katie. Katie handed her the card.

"You made this?" Charlotte asked.

Katie nodded. "I colored the pictures too."

"It's pretty," Charlotte said.

The boy just stood there next to the food, polite but looking bored.

"Did you find out what was wrong?" Margaret asked quietly.

"No," I said. "Not yet."

Margaret touched my arm. "I'm sorry. Just know that you're in our prayers, and just let me know if there's anything we can do—I've got a house full of babysitters."

"You're very kind," I said, genuinely moved by her graciousness.

She called out, "Come on, Katie, it's time to go. Charlotte needs her rest."

Margaret shepherded her children to the front door, and once they were outside, Katie and her brother sprinted home. Margaret paused in the doorway. "By the way, just after you left Friday, a young man came by your house. He saw us in the yard, so he came over and asked if we'd seen you. I told him what had happened, about the ambulance and all, I hope you don't mind. He seemed like a nice man.

He asked me to tell you that he'll come back next week. I think he said his name is Matthew."

"Thank you," I said. "We had . . ." I suddenly felt embarrassed. "An appointment."

"Well, he seemed very concerned when I told him about Charlotte, so I figured you must be close."

"He's just an acquaintance," I said. "But thank you."

"I hope you enjoy the casserole. It's my George's favorite, but some people don't care for broccoli."

"I love broccoli," I said. "I should eat more of it."

"I tell my kids that. Doesn't help that our new president hates broccoli."

"I guess not everyone's a fan."

"I marked the dishes with masking tape. Don't worry about bringing them back. I'll send one of the kids by in a few days."

"Thank you. You're very sweet."

"Just being neighborly," she said. "Have a good Sabbath."

I watched her walk down the sidewalk, then waved again and shut the door. It was a real luxury to have a homemade meal that had been prepared by someone besides me. Outside of McDonald's, or the hospital's café, I couldn't remember the last time I had eaten someone else's cooking.

"Are you hungry, Char?"

She shook her head. "My stomach hurts when I eat."

"Just have a little then, okay?"

She walked over dutifully. "Okay."

I had just dished up our plates and taken a few bites when the doorbell rang. "I'll be right back," I said to Charlotte.

I opened the door to find Matthew standing on our front porch.

"Your neighbor told me there was an ambulance here," he said. "Is Charlotte all right?"

"Yes." I brushed the hair from my face. "How did you know my daughter's name?"

"Your neighbor."

"I'm sorry about missing you the other night. We had to rush her to the hospital."

"I understand completely. What happened?"

"She had a seizure."

"I'm sorry," he said. "I really am."

"The thing is, if I hadn't been here, I don't know what would have happened." I looked at him sadly. "I can't take a chance with her right now."

"What do you mean?"

"I'm sorry. I know I said I would go out with you, but it's just not the right time. Not now."

Like before, he seemed unaffected by my dismissal. "How old is Charlotte?"

"What?"

"Right now, how old is she?"

"She's six."

"Six," he said. "You don't know . . ." he stopped mid-sentence. "Did she eat something before the seizure?"

I couldn't figure out why he was asking me this. "She was eating dinner."

"What was she eating?"

"Ramen noodles."

How did he know?

✦ Beth Cardall's Diary ✦

He nodded. "Of course. Beth, you need to trust me, this is very important. I want you to tell the doctors that you think Charlotte has a disease called celiac sprue. Have you ever heard of that?"

"No."

"Celiac sprue is an allergic reaction to gluten. The seizure could have been a result of eating the noodles. She's probably been losing weight and doesn't like eating lately, does she?"

"How did you know that?"

"It goes with the disease. Whatever you do, do not feed her anything with gluten."

"I don't know what gluten is."

"It's a protein found in grains like wheat, rye and barley. Just look at the ingredients on the package, it should say. Just don't feed her anything with wheat, rye or barley. Promise me."

I looked at him quizzically. "Are you a doctor?"

"No, I just have a lot of experience with this."

I had no idea what to think of him. "I appreciate your trying to help, but you've never even seen my daughter. Several doctors examining her couldn't tell what was wrong. They thought she might have Whipple's or Crohn's disease."

"No, she doesn't," he said flatly. "She's celiac. Doctors misdiagnose this all the time." His expression turned more serious. "Beth, don't let yourself get in the way of Charlotte's well-being. I'm not asking you to take any great leap of faith, here. Just try what I said for a couple days and see if she stops having problems. That's it. If that works, then go for a whole week. You have nothing to lose—she has nothing to lose."

"I need to talk to the doctors first."

"Great, ask your doctors. Tell them that you think it might be celiac sprue and see what they say." He took a pen from his coat pocket. "Do you have some paper?" Before I could answer, he spotted a flier for snow removal that someone had left on our porch. He picked it up and wrote on the back, spelling out the letters as he penned them, "C-e-l-i-a-c s-p-r-u-e. Celiac sprue." He handed me the paper. "The doctors will know what it is. Trust me. Everything will be all right. I promise." He looked at me for a moment, then said, "I'm going to be gone for a while. Maybe a few weeks. But I'll be back." He started to turn.

Something about his promise made me angry. "You can't promise me that everything will be okay," I said sharply. "That's not a promise you can keep."

He turned back with a peculiar, knowing smile. "You'd be surprised at what promises I can keep."

He walked out to the curb where his car, an old VW Beetle, was parked. I stood on the porch, silently watching him go. He opened his door, then shouted to me. "Trust, Bethany. Trust." He climbed into his car and drove away.

CHAPTER

Sixteen

I suppose I felt like King Naaman in the Bible being told by the prophet Elisha to wash seven times in the river Jordan and be healed. Honestly, I didn't know what to think. I had no reason to trust this man, none whatsoever, but I was taken by the forcefulness of his conviction. I shut the door and went back inside. Charlotte was at the table clumsily buttering a piece of bread. I looked at her a moment then said, "Honey, let's not eat that."

"How come?"

"I just want to try something. We're going to be very careful about what you eat the next few days. Okay?"

"Okay."

"Let me get you something else." I looked at what Margaret had brought. Casserole, bread, dessert. Everything had wheat. I opened up a can of peaches and poured them into a bowl. "Here you go, honey."

"Thanks, Mom."

While Charlotte finished eating, I went to my bedroom, shut the door and called the hospital. Dr. Hansen, who had watched over Charlotte on Friday, was on shift, but he was with a patient. I left my number with a nurse. It was several hours later, as I was putting Charlotte down to bed, that the phone rang. I kissed her goodnight, then answered the phone. It was Dr. Hansen returning my call.

"Doctor, I don't know if you remember me. I came in Friday night with my little girl, Charlotte. She had a seizure."

"Of course. How is she?"

I suddenly felt a little awkward. "She's been about the same. I hope you don't think I'm crazy, but a friend thought he knew what might be wrong." I looked at the paper Matthew had written on. "Could she have celiac sprue?"

The doctor was quiet a moment. Then he said: "That would explain her stomach and weight problems. There are even some studies that suggest a link between celiac sprue and seizures. Your friend may be right."

Honestly, I hadn't expected this response. "Oh. So what do I do?"

"Celiac sprue is an autoimmune disease that's triggered by the protein gluten, which is pretty common in our diet. It's found in things like bread, pasta, cookies—anything made with wheat, barley and a few other grains. If I were you, I would go a week without giving her anything with gluten and see what happens. Do you have a pediatrician?"

"Yes. Dr. Benton at the Mid-Valley Clinic."

"He can tell you more about the disease. Let's hope that's what it is."

"Thank you, doctor."

"You're welcome. Have a good night." He hung up.

Didn't expect that, I thought.

✳

Monday, Charlotte and I stayed home again. I sat down and made a list of foods she could eat. Designing a menu without gluten was like building a house without wood—it can be done, but it takes some planning.

Charlotte didn't have a stomachache the entire day and that evening seemed to be more active than usual. The next morning I woke to find her sitting up in our bed. It was the first time in more than a year that I hadn't had to wake her. "Can I watch cartoons?"

I rubbed the sleep from my eyes, surprised to be woken by something other than my radio alarm. "How long have you been awake?"

"I dunno."

I looked over at the clock. It was eight minutes before seven. "How are you feeling, honey?"

"Good."

"No headache or tummy ache?"

She shook her head. "Nope. Can I?"

"Yes, you may."

I got up and turned the television on for her, then shut off my alarm clock before it went off. After showering and dressing I made Charlotte breakfast. Out of habit I put a piece of bread in the toaster but stopped myself and scrambled an egg instead. As she was eating, I called Dr. Benton's office. The clinic didn't open until nine and I had expected to just leave a message, but fortuitously Dr. Benton was in the clinic early that morning and answered the phone. I briefed him about our emergency run to the hospital and then, a little more confidently, asked him if Charlotte's ailments could be celiac sprue.

"It makes sense," he said. "I should have thought of that myself. But it wouldn't be the first time a doctor missed it. Celiac sprue is hard to diagnose."

"How would that affect her?"

"When someone with celiac eats something containing gluten, the gluten causes a reaction that damages the intestine and makes the body unable to absorb nutrients, which, of course, can lead to a whole host of nasty problems—weight loss, anemia, malnutrition, seizures, even cancer."

"Cancer?"

"It can if untreated. Hold on a second, I think I have some material here on it." He left the phone for a moment, then returned. "Symptoms of celiac sprue include gastrointestinal problems such as diarrhea, abdominal pain and bloating. Other related symptoms include irritability, anemia, upset stomach, joint pain, skin rash, etc. Celiac can cause malabsorption, with such symptoms as weight loss, stunted growth, cramps, fatigue, and weakness."

"That sounds like Charlotte," I said softly. "So what is the treatment?"

"Well, it's simple but hard—just don't eat gluten. If you can come by the clinic, I have some brochures on celiac I think you'll find helpful. This brochure here even has some meal-planning suggestions."

"I'll try to make it by this afternoon."

"Good. Hopefully we'll figure out what this thing is and get her better."

"Thank you, Doctor." I was about to hang up when Dr. Benton asked, "By the way, how did you figure this out?"

"A friend of mine said he had a lot of experience with it."

"Well, you should bake him a cake," he said, then added, "Just make sure Charlotte doesn't eat any of it."

I hung up the phone. *Curiouser and curiouser.*

CHAPTER

Seventeen

Einstein said that the most beautiful thing
we can experience is the mysterious.
Perhaps that's why Matthew's so beautiful to me.

✦ Beth Cardall's Diary ✦

It was an hour after sunset when Roxanne dropped by the house to visit. After Charlotte was in bed, we went out to the kitchen. I made us some decaf coffee and we sat at the table.

"Charlotte looks like she's doing better."

"She is. We're trying a new diet. The doctors think she might be allergic to gluten."

"Finally they have something. When did they figure that out?"

I took a slow sip of coffee. "That's the thing—*they* didn't. Matthew did."

"Matthew? Mr. Soap Opera?"

"The same. He came over last Sunday. I was still a bit in shock from Friday, so I was explaining to him why it wasn't a good time for me to see him, when he tells me that Charlotte has this celiac disease and is allergic to gluten."

"How did he know that?"

"I have no idea."

"But he was right?"

I shrugged. "She hasn't complained of a headache or stomachache since I changed her diet. She has more energy than

I've seen in years and even her skin color has changed. She looks healthy again."

"That's amazing."

I shook my head. "Honestly, Rox, it was so curious."

"How's that?"

"Well, it wasn't like he was guessing at her disease; it was more like he knew what was wrong. He was just so confident. In fact, he asked something that was a little strange."

"What's that?"

"He asked me how old Charlotte was. I thought it was a little random, but when I told him, he said, 'She's only six, you don't know . . . ' And then he stopped, mid-sentence. It's weird, but I think he was going to say, 'you don't know *yet*.' "

I took another sip of coffee. "I don't know what to think."

"Maybe he's an angel," Roxanne said, then added, "Sure looks like one."

I rolled my eyes. "I called the hospital to ask if it could be this celiac thing, and the doctor was impressed with the diagnosis. Then, yesterday, I called Dr. Benton and asked him. He agreed that celiac was a distinct possibility."

"That's crazy. So do they give her drugs for that?"

"No, it's an allergic reaction to gluten, so we have to change her diet."

"What's gluten?"

"That's what I asked. It's a protein found in grains, like wheat."

"You mean she can't eat anything with flour? No cake, cookies, pizza?"

"No."

Roxanne grimaced. "That's awful."

"Not as awful as what she's been going through. And at least it's manageable. Untreated, it can cause cancer and a lot of other problems, even seizures. It's possible that that's what happened Friday night when I gave Charlotte that bowl of Ramen—it triggered a seizure. Here I was trying to make her eat all these carbohydrates so she would gain weight, and I was really just poisoning her. So much for the Mother-of-the-Year Award."

"Girl, you're the best mother I know. You didn't know. The doctors didn't even know. So maybe Mr. Gorgeous is secretly a doctor."

"I thought you said he was an angel."

"Maybe he's both. No matter what he is, you owe him. What are you going to do to thank him?"

"I don't know," I said, resting my head in my hands. "I haven't thought about it."

"Well, you better start. When do you see him again?"

"I don't know that either. He said he was leaving town for a while. He said he'd be back in a couple weeks."

"Good," Roxanne said. "It will give you some time to figure out how to properly thank him. And I'm tellin' you, sister, it better be good. You let this one off the hook, I'm revoking your fishing license."

CHAPTER

Eighteen

Matthew met Charlotte today.
There was a discernible energy between them.
I don't know if this should please or concern me.

✦ Beth Cardall's Diary ✦

Matthew didn't come back that week, and by the end of the next week I began to worry that he might not return at all. Roxanne kept assuring me he'd be back, but I think that secretly she was also worried. After all I had done to push him away, I was surprised at how disappointed I was.

On the bright side, Charlotte just kept doing better. She was back in school, and her teacher, Miss Rossi, stopped me one day after school in the parking lot to tell me how miraculous the change had been. "She's like a new girl," she said. "I just wish she could share some of that energy."

Thursday afternoon I was in the living room reading when a navy blue BMW with dealer plates pulled into my driveway. Other than the family who owned the cleaners, I didn't know anyone with that nice of a car, and my first thought was that it had just pulled into my driveway to turn around, but it stopped. The driver's door opened and Matthew stepped out. He was dressed in tan corduroy jeans and a thick, leather bomber jacket with Wayfarer sunglasses. He looked like something out of a men's fashion magazine. Seeing him made me happy.

I set down my book and met him at the door before he rang the bell. He had removed his sunglasses.

"What happened to your VW?" I asked.

"I traded up," he said. "The bug kept breaking down."

"It's good to see you," I said.

He smiled. "I'm glad to hear that. So how is everyone? How's Charlotte?"

I put my hands on my hips. "She's doing well. Actually, she's doing amazingly well. But I think you already knew she'd be better."

"Knew? No. But I hoped."

"Hope," I repeated. "I've been in short supply of that lately. I don't know how to thank you. My friend Rox said it better be something good."

He grinned. "You should listen to her. So let me think about this. What's the best way to thank a man who potentially saved your daughter's life? The mind reels."

I cocked my head. "Within reason."

"Well, considering the recent change in circumstances, if your moratorium on dating has been lifted, a simple date will suffice."

"Gladly. When would you like to go out?"

"You said weekends are good. How about tomorrow night?"

"I'll need to find a babysitter."

"Charlotte can come," he said.

"No, I'd rather keep her out of my dating life. I think it would be confusing to her."

He nodded. "Wise."

"So, what do you want to do?" I asked.

"I don't care. Just spend time with you. Dinner and talking sounds good."

"That sounds good to me too. You should probably give me your phone number, just in case something happens again."

"Unfortunately, I don't have a phone. But I can call you, if you'll give me your number."

"I'll write it down. Can you come inside for a moment?"

"Of course." He followed me inside the foyer.

"You can wait here. My kitchen's a little messy."

"No problem."

I found a pen in the kitchen, but it didn't work, so I rooted through drawers for some other writing implement, ending up with one of Charlotte's crayons. I found a note pad in the pantry and scrawled down my phone number. As I walked back to the foyer, I saw Charlotte standing close to Matthew. He was crouched down and moving away from her, as if he had touched or hugged her. I wasn't sure what I was seeing.

"Charlotte," I said. "I thought you were in bed, honey."

"I heard the door open," she said, "I came to see who was here."

I looked back and forth between them. I couldn't explain it, but there was a strange energy. I wasn't sure in the dim lighting, but Matthew's eyes seemed wet. "Matthew, this is my daughter Charlotte."

He extended his hand to her. "Nice to meet you, Charlotte. I'm Matthew."

"Nice to meet you, Matthew."

"Mr. Matthew," I said. "Now go back to bed."

"Okay." She waved at him. "Bye, Mr. Matthew."

"Good night, Charlotte."

She ran back to the bedroom.

"She's a very sweet girl," he said to me. "She looks well."

"Thanks to you."

"She's going to be a very beautiful woman someday. I guarantee it." Then he looked at me. "Like her mother."

"Thank you." I handed him the paper. "Here you are. The top number is my phone number at the house and the bottom number is the cleaners."

"I'll call you tomorrow."

"I'll look forward to it."

"Well, good night." He turned to go.

As he walked out the front door I said, "Matthew."

"Yes."

"How did you know? About Charlotte?"

He shrugged. "Lucky guess."

"But you weren't guessing. You told me to trust you."

He just looked at me for a moment. "I recognized the symptoms from what you told me." He saluted. "Good night, Beth."

"Good night, Matthew."

When he was in his car, I shut the door and leaned against it. There was something mysterious about this man. Something sweet but mysterious. What was I missing?

CHAPTER

Nineteen

*Some relationships need to be pounded into place
with a sledge hammer, while others effortlessly fall
into place as if made to fit. Matthew fits as comfortably as
a pair of Hush Puppy loafers.*

*(Rox once told me that the brand name Hush Puppies
came when the shoe company's president was eating a
southern dinner of fried corn "hush puppies" and asked the
waitress why they were so called. She replied, "Because
farmers throw them to the hounds to quiet their barking
dogs." Barking dogs was, back then, an idiom for sore feet,
and a star was born.*

*Or maybe Rox was just making that up.
With Rox one never quite knows where truth ends
and imagination begins.)*

✦ Beth Cardall's Diary ✦

I called Roxanne as soon as Matthew left to see if Jan could babysit. As I expected, she was relieved to hear of his return. "I knew he'd be back," she said. "I told you, didn't I?"

"Right as usual," I said.

"Well, come hell or high water you're going out with that man. Jan's out with her friends right now, but if she can't sit, you can just bring Charlotte on by the house. Ray and I aren't doing anything."

"Thanks, Rox."

"My pleasure, baby. I just love a new romance. My candle may be flickering, but I can still warm myself by your flame."

Jan wasn't busy Friday night, and in spite of her previous experience with Charlotte, she was happy to babysit. As usual, she came a little early. I hugged her at the door. "I never thanked you for your help last time."

"I was glad to help. Sure scared me, though."

"That makes two of us."

"Where's our girl?"

"She's in her bedroom."

"Not anymore," Jan said as Charlotte came running toward her.

"Jan!"

"Hi, sweetie. Wow, you look as bubbly as a shaken soda. Where'd you get all that energy?"

"I'm celiac," she said.

"You're what?"

"She's allergic to wheat," I said. "I've made a list for you of things she can eat. Will it be a problem if we're out late?"

"No worries, Mrs. C. I've got an essay I need to write."

"Wanna play with Molly?" Charlotte asked.

Jan grabbed her hand. "You know I do."

The two of them ran off. I went and checked myself in the mirror again, and a few minutes later Matthew's car pulled into the driveway. He came to the door holding a small bouquet of flowers that he surrendered to me.

"Gerbera daisies," I said. "I love Gerbera daisies. Thank you. Let me put them in some water. Come in."

While he was waiting for me, Charlotte walked back out to the door dragging Jan behind her. "This is my Mom's new friend. Hi, Mr. Matthew."

"Hello, Miss Charlotte," Matthew said.

"I'm Jan," Jan said. "Charlotte's babysitter."

"So you're Jan," he said with a slight lilt. "I've heard so much about you."

"Really? From whom?"

There was an awkward pause, then he said to Charlotte, "I brought you something. Do you like peanut butter cups?"

"Yes."

"It's all yours. Gluten-free."

"Thank you, Mr. Matthew."

"You two have a good night. It's nice to meet you, Jan."

I put the flowers in a vase, then walked back out. "Jan, we'll be leaving now. Bedtime is nine."

"Have fun," she said. "Don't worry about a thing."

"Are you taking my mommy to dinner?" Charlotte asked Matthew.

He crouched down to her height. "Yes, I am. Is that okay?"

"Don't make her cry."

"Okay," I said, "that's enough of that."

Matthew winked at her. "I promise I'll try not to."

"Good night, honey," I said, and kissed her. "Go to bed when Jan tells you."

Matthew and I walked out to his car. "Sorry about that," I said when the door shut. "She's a little protective."

"I wonder where she gets that," he said.

"So bribing the child with candy. Trying to make her like you?"

"Whatever works."

"Oh, by the way," I said. "Don't make me cry."

He grinned. "I'll do my best." He opened my door, then walked around and climbed in. "I hope you're hungry. I made reservations at a little place called the Five Alls."

I looked at him with surprise. "That's my favorite restaurant."

"Good," he said. "Then if my company stinks, at least you'll enjoy the food."

✦

The Five Alls is a charming English-themed restaurant off Foothill Drive on the east bench of the Salt Lake Valley. It was the backdrop to some of my fondest memories: my first prom, Marc and my engagement, our first anniversary, and Charlotte's first day of school.

The hostess sat us at a small table for two in a secluded back room near a fireplace.

"In all the years I've been coming here, I've never sat back here," I said.

"It's a bit more private," he said. "Perfect for talking."

A few moments later a waitress walked back to our table. She was immediately attracted to Matthew. "My name is Samantha, I'll be taking care of you tonight," she said, looking only at him.

You wish, I thought.

"Hello, Samantha," Matthew said. "So what's good tonight?"

"It's all good," she said. "Here are your menus. We have a few specials tonight. The Halibut Oscar, with crab and Hollandaise sauce, is one of my personal favorites, and the filet Roquefort, which is a six-ounce filet mignon topped with bacon, blue cheese and a burgundy wine sauce. And for dessert we have our seasonal English trifle and raisin-bread pudding."

"Sounds delicious," I said, letting her know I was there. "Thank you."

She furtively glanced at me. "I'll give you a moment to look over the menu. May I bring you something to drink?"

"I'll have a glass of Merlot," I said.

"The same," Matthew said.

"Very good. I'll be right back." She smiled again at Matthew and walked away.

When she left the room I said, "That was awkward."

"What was?"

"The way she was fawning over you."

"You're just imagining things. So what are you going to have?"

I lifted the menu to look it over, even though I always ordered the same thing.

Suddenly, Matthew said, "Wait, may I order for you?"

I looked up at him. "You want to order for me?"

"Sure. I'm kind of an expert at this."

I closed the menu. "Okay. Let's see how you do."

A few moments later the waitress returned with our drinks. She turned to me. "Are you ready to order?"

"Ask him," I said. "He's in charge."

"Yes, we are ready. My friend would like the filet Roquefort, medium rare, the baked potato with sour cream and chives, the melon prosciutto appetizer and the house salad with blue cheese, wait, Thousand Island?" He looked at me. "No, blue cheese dressing."

The waitress looked back at me for confirmation. He was

dead-on, right down to the salad dressing. "That's what I'll have."

"And you, sir?"

"I would like the king crab legs, baked potato with Norshire garnish and the cream of mushroom soup. And blue cheese dressing with my salad."

"Very well," she said. She took our menus and walked away.

"Sounds like you've been here before," I said.

"A few times. So how did I do?"

"It was a gutsy move ordering red meat for a woman."

He smiled. "You look like a woman who can handle red meat."

"I don't know what that means, but I'll take it as a compliment. Yes, you did well. That's what I always order. So, are you psychic?"

"It's kind of a party trick," he said. "Speaking of which, tell me about yourself."

I laughed. "I can't believe you just used that as a segue. So your psychic powers haven't told you everything about me. What do you want to know?"

"What is it like working at a dry cleaner?"

"Really? That's what you want to know?"

"Why not?"

"Okay. It's a job. Not a lot of excitement, but it almost pays the bills, and I get my dry cleaning done for free. And if I actually wore something nice enough to need dry cleaning, that would be a real perk."

"I can see why you work there," he said.

"Now you're just being mean. So what do you do?"

"Stalk, mostly. And diagnose enigmatic diseases."

"I believe you."

"Actually, I'm kind of between jobs right now."

"And you just bought a new BMW?"

"I'm financially stable."

"That's good," I said. "So, what did you do when you were employed?"

"I was a financial advisor. I help high-income clientele with their investment portfolios. People like you."

"That's me, all right. So I have a question. The first time we met . . ."

"The head butt," he said.

"Right. The head butt. I wondered what a man like you was doing alone at a 7-Eleven on Christmas morning."

"A man like *what*?"

"Just a very handsome, well-put-together man."

"I could ask you the same thing—except for the man part."

"I just needed buttermilk."

"Well, other than looking for someone to head butt, the answer is not that exciting. I had just moved to Utah and I hadn't done any serious grocery shopping yet, so I ran out of coffee. Being Christmas Day, I went to the only place I could think of that was open. And then, voilà, this angel walks in and transforms me into a bumbling, head-butting fool."

"Oh, I looked like an angel all right."

"More than you know."

"Do you have family?"

"My parents live in Toledo, Ohio. I have a younger brother who lives in Maryland. He's very smart. He speaks seven languages and works for the NSA." He lifted his glass and smiled at me. "I'm pretty sure that he's a spy, but he won't admit it. Actually, I was hoping to spend Christmas with my parents, but this year it just seemed a little too . . ." He seemed like he was searching for the right word. "Far."

The waitress came over with a pitcher of water and topped off our glasses. She smiled at Matthew. "I'll be right back with your first course."

"Thank you," he said.

I leaned forward. "Don't take this wrong, but it's hard for me to believe that a man as handsome and persistent as you isn't married."

The playfulness in his countenance suddenly vanished. "I was," he said simply.

"Was?"

His expression changed. "I lost her. She died of cancer."

"I'm sorry," I said.

"Me too," he said sadly. "She was everything to me. Sweet, smart, beautiful." He stopped, overcome with emotion.

"I'm really sorry, that must have been painful."

When he could speak, he said, "It was like having my heart amputated and still having to live." He breathed in deeply, then exhaled. "But you understand, don't you? You lost your husband to cancer."

"I don't know," I said. "It wasn't quite the same."

"Why is that?"

I frowned. "I don't know how much I want to share."

"That's okay," he said. "Whatever you're comfortable with."

I looked into Matthew's eyes and all I saw was sympathy. "I caught him cheating on me. It was just a few weeks after that that he was diagnosed with terminal cancer. So I stuck with him. I even forgave him. Things between us were good until a few weeks before he died, when he confessed to having multiple affairs. Nearly a dozen."

Matthew groaned. "A serial cheater. I'm sorry."

"Yeah, me too," I said, surprised I had opened up so much. "The thing is, I didn't have a clue about any of it. I was living in this fantasyland where life was good and family was enough. I guess I was wrong."

Matthew shook his head. "You weren't wrong. Family is enough." He looked into my eyes. "So how are you doing?"

I took a deep breath, exhaling slowly. "The thing is, broken vows are like broken mirrors. They leave those who held to them bleeding and staring at fractured images of themselves."

"That's very poetic."

"A broken heart will do that."

Just then the waitress arrived carrying a large platter. "Here's your first course. Swedish meatballs, our dill, sourdough breadsticks with homemade clam dip and a banana "shrub" to cleanse your palate. I'll be back in a moment with your salads."

When she walked away, I took a sip of wine, then speared a meatball from the pewter dish with a tiny fork.

"I love those," Matthew said, watching me.

"How could you not?" I replied. "I love coming here." I finished chewing, then said, "So, I'm not really sure how old you are. What year did you graduate?"

He looked down for a moment. "Uh, class of . . . eighty."

I smiled. "That sounded like a guess. Are you sure?"

"I'm pretty sure."

"So I'm older than you."

"How much older?" he asked.

"Two years."

He rubbed his chin. "You are old."

"It's not too late to back out," I said.

"I'm afraid it is. We've already ordered."

I grinned. "So, do you know what I miss most about the old days?"

"We're still too young to say *the old days*," he said.

"Okay, then the seventies. I miss the music from back then. It was fun. None of this rap, kill-cops stuff."

"I like rap," he said. "Some of it at least. But you're right, music was more innocent back then."

"What was your favorite band?"

He dipped a breadstick into the clam dip. "I don't know if I had a favorite. I'm pretty eclectic. How about you?"

"Let's see. Queen, Supertramp, Peaches and Herb."

"Peaches and Herb?" he said laughing. "There's a name for you."

"They were one-hit wonders. You remember them, don't you?" I started singing, "Reunited and it feels so good . . ."

He laughed. "I guess I missed that."

"You really missed out. Of course, like everyone else, I was madly in love with the Bee Gees. How about you?"

He shook his head. "I'm not familiar with them."

I looked at him incredulously. "With the Bee Gees?"

He shrugged.

"The Bee Gees," I said again as if he hadn't heard me. "You know, the brothers Gibb. *Saturday Night Fever*?"

He still gazed at me blankly.

"Come on, 'Staying Alive,' 'Night Fever,' 'Too Much Heaven.' None of that rings a bell?"

"Nada."

"You've got to be kidding me. How could you have missed the Bee Gees? 'Night Fever' was the biggest song of the year."

He shrugged. "I wasn't much into heavy metal."

I burst out laughing. "Heavy metal? They're disco. How could you have been alive and missed the whole disco era?"

He thought about it for a moment, then said, "Lucky?"

I laughed again. "Wow. Where are you from? Outer Mongolia?"

"Actually, Capri."

"Capri?"

He nodded. "It's an island off the coast of southern Italy. We didn't have much of a disco thing going on up there. I'm pretty sure there wasn't a mirror ball on the whole island."

I took a drink of wine. "You're Italian, then."

"I have dual citizenship. My father is from southern Italy. My mother was a southern belle from Atlanta. So I'm a southerner on both sides. Actually, I was born in Capri but lived in Sorrento until I was thirteen when we came to the States with my father's job."

I realized that I didn't even know his last name. "What is your last name?"

"Principato."

"Definitely sounds Italian. Do you still speak Italian?"

"*Ma certo, bella.*"

"I have no idea what you just said, but it was very pretty."

"*La bella lingua,*" he said. "It's the only language in the world that was invented by a poet."

"Really?"

He nodded. "Dante."

"Italian," I said again. "That explains your beautiful eyes."

He smiled shyly.

"Tell me more about yourself," I said.

"Well, something strange happened to me the other day. Actually it was about a month ago. I heard this scratching at my front door, so I opened the door, but there was no one there. However, I noticed a snail on the doorstep, so I picked it up and threw it across the street.

"Then, a week ago I heard that same scratching sound at the door again. I got up and opened the door. Again, no one was there. But there was that snail again. He looked up at me and said, 'What was that about?' "

I burst out laughing. "That is the dumbest thing I've ever heard."

"I know. It's great, isn't it?"

"It is," I conceded.

✦

The night was different than I thought it would be. Matthew was different than I thought he would be. He was funnier, smarter, simpler. We laughed and joked and I hadn't had that much fun since I could remember.

We finished eating around ten and then just drank coffee and talked until eleven. Then he paid the bill and drove me home. He turned off his car in the driveway and turned to me. "So, how did I do? Passing grade?"

"I'd give you a C+."

"C+? That's not good. But it's still a passing grade?"

"Barely. The snail story was a little sketchy, but the meal was great and I'm feeling generous, so I will allow a makeup."

"Thank you. When can I try again?"

"Soon," I said. "Hopefully."

He smiled. "How about I come over Sunday and make dinner. I will make you my *soon-to-be-famous* fried rice."

"Chinese, not Italian?"

"The only Italian dishes I make are pasta dishes."

"What's wrong with pasta?"

"Charlotte can't eat it."

"Oh." I was impressed that he had thought of that and felt foolish that I hadn't. "Chinese sounds terrific. What do you need from me?"

"You're in charge of drinks."

"It's a deal."

He came around and opened my door, then walked me

to the front porch. We stopped in front of the door. "Thank you for going out with me," he said. "It was fun. You're a very interesting woman."

"Interesting," I said. "I like that. It was my pleasure." I looked into his eyes. "May I tell you something personal?"

"Of course."

"That was the best night I've had in the last two years." His eyes shone when I said that and he looked even more attractive to me than when I first met him.

"I'm glad." He leaned forward and kissed my cheek. "Good night, Beth."

"Good night, Matthew."

He walked back to his car. I leaned back against the door as he drove away. Then I went inside. Jan was at the kitchen table doing her homework.

"Hi, Mrs. C. How was your evening?"

"Perfect," I said, a broad smile crossing my face. "Just perfect."

CHAPTER

Twenty

*Finding real love is like finding a hundred dollar bill
in a Kmart parking lot—and about as likely.*

✦ Beth Cardall's Diary ✦

The next morning at work Roxanne was as wired as a hummingbird on caffeine. "How was it? Jan said you said it was perfect. Tell me everything. Full report."

A content smile crossed my face. "He was wonderful."

"What did you do with Mr. Wonderful?"

"He took me to my favorite restaurant. We talked. We laughed a lot. He is very sweet and funny and very romantic."

"Girl, I told you so, didn't I?"

"And he's Italian."

"Grand slam."

"There was only one thing I didn't like about the date."

"He mentioned an old girlfriend," Roxanne said. "He wore white socks."

"What? White socks? No, the only thing I didn't like is that he didn't kiss me. Maybe he saw me up close and changed his mind about me."

"Honey, stop that. You know you're gorgeous. And after how hard you tried to scare him off, he was probably just being careful. Or being a gentleman. And heaven knows we could use a few more of those."

"Well, he's coming over Sunday night to make fried rice."

Roxanne nodded contently. "And he cooks. You were right, it may be too good to be true. So let's get down to bare knuckles. How many times has he been married, and is he gainfully employed?"

"He *was* married, once, and he *was* employed. He's between jobs right now."

Roxanne grimaced. "Oh, not good."

"About which."

"Divorced I can handle, but the 'between jobs' thing sounds a little dodgy."

"I think it's okay. He's financially stable, evident from the new BMW he was driving. He used to be a financial advisor, but he's looking for something more meaningful."

"Money and conscience. So tell me this—he's Italian, gorgeous, nice, financially stable and can cook. What woman in her right mind would leave him?"

"His wife died of cancer."

She looked strangely happy to hear this. "Oh."

"I saw this very beautiful side of him. He was still mourning her."

"Two broken hearts who still believe in the promise of love. Beth, this is a gift from heaven, he could be your soul mate."

"I can't believe I'm saying this, but do you think it's too soon to be falling in love?"

"When did you know you wanted to marry Marc?"

"Second date."

She nodded. "You know when you're out shopping and you find that pair of red high heels that practically kicks you from the shelf?"

I laughed. "You're comparing guys with shoes?"

"Well, I know it's not fair to the shoes, but it's essentially the same thing. When you know, you know."

"You're a nut."

"That's why you love me. So he's coming over tomorrow night?"

I smiled at the thought of it. "Tomorrow night."

"And you're not worried about Charlotte being there?"

"I should be, but I'm not. He's even cooking something that Charlotte can eat."

"I am so pleased for you. You discovered what's wrong with Charlotte, you found a nice, financially secure guy you like being with—I'd say things are finally looking up."

I nodded happily. "It feels like it. You think my luck has finally changed?"

"Yes. And it's about time, I say."

"I hope," I said. "I hope."

CHAPTER

Twenty-one

Something you lost will soon turn up.

✦ Fortune Cookie ✦

Sunday evening Matthew rang the bell around five-thirty. I opened the door to find him holding three large paper sacks.

"How did you ring the bell?" I asked.

"With my elbow."

"Come in," I said. "I'll take one of those."

"I wasn't sure what ingredients you had so I just bought everything."

We carried the sacks into the kitchen. He took off his coat, then we began emptying the sacks onto the counter. There was rice, soy sauce, carrots, onions, eggs, chicken breasts, ham steak, garlic and scallions. In addition, there were fortune cookies, three pairs of chopsticks, three rice hats and a plastic baggie filled with grass.

"What's this?" I said holding up the baggie.

"Grass. I didn't know where to find hay."

"You cook with hay?"

"No. The Chinese New Year is next Friday. And it is the year of the horse, hence the hay which, in our case, is grass."

He walked over and set a rice hat on my head. "You have to wear this. Health department regulations." He tied the ribbon beneath my chin. "Perfect."

"Then you have to wear yours," I said. I picked one up, put it on his head, and fastened the ribbon. "You still look Italian."

"Thank you," he said.

There was another hat about half the size of the ones we wore. "You even brought a little one for Charlotte."

"We didn't want to leave her out of the fun. So where is Charlotte?"

"She's next door at her friend's house. But I called just before you came, so she'll be home in a few minutes."

"Great. Let's get started."

"What do you want me to do?" I asked, sure I looked stupid under the hat.

"You got the drinks?"

"It's not very Chinese, but I made lemonade. There's also beer and soda in the fridge. What else can I do to help?"

"Can you cook the rice?"

"I'm on it."

"Where do you keep your knives?"

"Knives are in that drawer. The cutting board is below the sink."

While I put the rice in the rice cooker, Matthew began dicing the carrots, garlic and onions. When he was done, he threw the vegetables into separate pans to sauté. Before long the kitchen smelled wonderful. Fumbling with chopsticks, I picked up one of his carrots from the pan, blew on it, then dropped it in my mouth. "Ooh, that's good," I said.

"I sauté all the vegetables in garlic butter. The garlic is key."

"I love garlic," I said. "Though usually not in the early dating phase."

"I disagree. Garlic is the great revealer. A relationship that can withstand garlic is worth pursuing."

"I'll keep that in mind."

"My secret to a great fried rice is to make sure that each ingredient tastes delicious on its own and don't overdo it on the soy sauce. People always overdo it on the soy sauce."

"I'll remember that."

"You don't need to," he said. "You can always just ask me to make it for you."

"I like that," I said.

He was cooking the chicken when Charlotte walked into the house. "Mom!"

"In here, sweetie."

She walked into the kitchen, then stopped and stared at us. "Hi, Mom, where'd you get the hat?"

"Mr. Matthew brought them. He brought one for you too. Do you want to put it on?"

Her face lit with excitement. "Uh-huh."

"Come here then." She ran to me and I set it on and tied it around her chin. She looked adorable. "Tell Mr. Matthew thank you."

"Thank you, Mr. Matthew."

"You're welcome, Miss Charlotte. We're celebrating the Chinese New Year. Do you know what that is?"

"We had enchiladas for New Year's," Charlotte said.

Matthew smiled. "You're a smart girl. Americans celebrate New Year's on January 1, but in China they have a different calendar and their first day of the year is different than ours."

I could see her thinking about this.

"Chinese New Year is a really big deal in China. It's their biggest holiday, like Christmas is here. All the people get together with their families and have big meals and share presents. At night they do fireworks, and in the morning the parents give their children red paper envelopes with money inside them."

"I would like that," Charlotte said.

"You know something else they do? Every year before the New Year begins, all the families clean their houses really well so they can sweep away all the bad luck from the old year and make room for good luck in the new year."

Charlotte nodded. "My room is clean."

"Then I guess we're ready." Matthew smiled at me. "I think we're all ready for a good year."

The rice was delicious, as was the conversation. Matthew had a genuine interest in Charlotte and seemed fascinated with everything she had to say. After the meal Matthew handed out fortune cookies and we broke them open.

"Something you lost will soon turn up," I read.

"That's intriguing," Matthew said. "Did you lose something?"

I looked at him and nodded. "I'm afraid so."

Just then Charlotte handed me her fortune. "Read mine."

" 'You will live a long and happy life.' That's a good one. What does yours say, Matthew?"

"A good reputation is something to prize." He looked at me and frowned. "That's not really a fortune. Fortune cookies should tell you something that will happen in the future, like, 'You're going to win the lottery,' or 'Your house will burn down.' I mean, what's the point of this?"

"Don't you think it's better not to know the future?" I asked.

"Why do you say that?"

"If we knew how everything was going to turn out we might not even try."

His countenance fell. "Maybe," he said. After a while he stood, then said, "All right, let's do the dishes."

"No, I'll do them later."

"It's a lot faster if—"

I reached over and put my finger on his lips. "I'm not in a hurry. I'd rather just spend the time with you. Let's go for a walk. Charlotte, do you mind being left alone for a few minutes? We're just walking down the street."

"It's okay, Mom."

We got our coats and walked outside into the frigid, February air. I was hoping he'd take my hand but he didn't, so after a minute I reached over and took his, intertwining my fingers with his. "That was a lot of fun," I said. "You make a mean fried rice."

"I told you I did." He looked at me. "So what you said about not knowing the future. Do you really mean that?"

I nodded. "I think so. I mean, if I had known that Marc was going to cheat on me, I'd never have married him."

He looked thoughtful. "I think you still would," he said. "Or you wouldn't have had Charlotte."

I thought about it. "You're right."

We walked a ways in silence. It was nice being with him. I loved his sense of humor. I loved the way he talked to me. After the second time around the block I said, "I better get back to Charlotte." I squeezed his hand and smiled. "I'm sorry I was so tough on you at first. Thank you for persevering. I don't know why you did it, but I'm grateful that you did."

"I had a hunch that you were worth persevering for."

"May I take you out next time?"

"I'd like that."

"When are you free?"

"I'm unemployed. I'm always free."

"Right, the life of a gentleman of leisure. How about next Friday?"

"Friday it is. What time?"

"For what I have in mind, we'll have to leave early. Like around four-thirtyish. We'll be gone until late."

"What do you have in mind?"

"It's a surprise."

"What should I dress for?"

"Dress very warm. Heavy coat, hat and gloves."

"Outdoor surprise. Nighttime snow thing?"

"Don't overanalyze it," I said. "You might ruin the surprise." I leaned against his car door, blocking his escape. It was cold and our breath froze in front of us. "Are you going to kiss me this time?" I asked.

He looked at me as if he was thinking it over. "Of course,"

he said. He leaned forward and gave me a quick peck on the lips.

My heart fell. Why didn't he really kiss me? Then a thought came to my mind that both comforted and stung— maybe he was still in love with his wife.

"You still miss her, don't you?"

"Because of the kiss," he said. "I'm sorry about that." He nodded slowly. "I'll miss her the rest of my life."

"What was she like?"

He looked at me sadly, then said softly, "She was a lot like you."

I looked down, unsure of what to say. Nearly a minute passed in silence. He spoke first, "You know your fortune— something you lost will soon turn up? What did you lose?"

I brushed my hair back from my face. "Trust."

"Do you think it will turn up?"

I looked into his eyes, then smiled. "I think the cookie was right."

CHAPTER

Twenty-two

I took Matthew on a romantic,
moonlight ride in a horse-drawn, open sleigh.
I feel like I'm living in a Hallmark commercial.
Whatever happened to too good to be true?

✦ Beth Cardall's Diary ✦

Friday afternoon I got off work at two-thirty to prepare for our date. I packed an overnight bag for Charlotte, then dropped her off at Roxanne's house to spend the night. I came back home and put together a picnic dinner of pitas stuffed with chicken salad, red grapes, two large pieces of butter-cream-frosted chocolate cake, a large thermos of steaming hot cocoa and a bowl of fresh homemade granola with cashews and cranberries to snack on during our drive to northern Utah.

I hoped he would like my surprise. When I was fourteen, I went with a group of friends on an outing to the Hardware Ranch; a 19,000-acre wildlife management area in eastern Cache Valley in northern Utah. (Cache Valley was named after the early mountainmen and trappers who used the area to cache their beaver pelts.)

We took a ride on a horse-drawn sleigh through the herd of more than six hundred elk that are fed on the ranch. Even at that age I remember thinking it would make for a romantic date. Our first year of marriage I told Marc about it. We were sitting on the sofa watching a Jazz basketball game on TV when I brought up the idea for our upcoming anniversary.

"Where's this place?"

"Hardware Ranch. It's just outside Logan."

"That's almost two hours away."

"Yes, but we'll be together. We can talk."

"I don't have that much to say," he said. "It sounds cold."

"That's part of the fun. We get to snuggle under a blanket."

He kissed me on the forehead. "We can do that here," he said and went back to the game.

I hoped Matthew would feel differently.

Matthew arrived at my home at four-thirty sharp. He pulled his car in next to mine, then climbed out wearing a thick wool coat and a cowboy hat. He looked a little like the Marlboro man, both masculine and boyishly cute.

"Nice hat," I said. "You look cute in it."

"Wasn't really going for 'cute,' but I'll take it."

I smiled. "Are you ready?"

"Absolutely. Shall I drive?"

"Okay, spoiler alert. Where we're going is two hours away through a snowy canyon."

We both looked at my old Nissan. "Maybe I should drive," he said.

"Good idea," I replied. "I still need to get a few things from the house." I ran inside, then came back a few moments later with my coat, a stocking cap, and a woven picnic basket.

He stared curiously at the basket. "That's a real picnic basket," he said. "Like on the Yogi Bear cartoons."

"Did they have Yogi Bear in Italy?"

"Of course." He opened my door for me. "After you," he said.

"Thank you," I said, sliding in.

He took the basket from me. "Should I put this in the trunk?"

"No. There's some granola in there for us to snack on, on the way."

"I'll just put it in the back." He set the basket on the back seat, then climbed in to the driver's seat and threw his hat in back. "Which way?"

"North. Like you were driving to Idaho."

"Idaho?"

"Don't worry, we're not going that far. We're going to Cache Valley."

"What's in Cache Valley?"

I looked at him and smiled. "My surprise."

The drive north was pleasant. We talked the whole way, though as I think back on it, I learned very little about Matthew. Every time I asked him a question about himself, he turned it back to me. I didn't so much sense that he was hiding anything, rather that he just had very little interest in talking about himself—a rare trait in most of the boys I'd dated. Nothing I revealed about myself seemed to surprise him. He asked a lot of questions about Charlotte, like how she did in school, special aptitudes, and if she had any boyfriends, which made me smile.

Around North Salt Lake we got caught in rush-hour traffic, but it thinned out by Layton, where we stopped at a McDonald's for Cokes. As we waited at the drive-in window, I reached in back and brought the bag of granola out of the basket. I opened the plastic bag and offered him some.

He popped a handful in his mouth. "Delicious. I love it when you make this," he said.

I looked at him quizzically. "What do you mean? I've never made it before."

He turned and looked at me then smiled. "I meant to say that I love it that you made it. I love granola."

The woman at the drive-thru window handed him our Cokes and he passed one on to me. Then we drove back to the highway. As we pulled from the ramp onto the highway, he said, "So when are you going to tell me where we're going?"

"I suppose it's about time. I made reservations for a moonlight sleigh ride at the Hardware Ranch."

I carefully watched his face for a reaction. To my relief, he smiled. "I've always wanted to go on a sleigh ride. Ever since I saw that old movie *Seven Brides for Seven Brothers.*"

"Really?"

"I really have. I just thought it seemed so romantic."

I stared at him in disbelief. He actually said "romantic" without smirking. Best of all, I could tell that he was sincere. He looked like an excited little boy on the way to an amusement park. *Where have you been all my life?* I thought.

As we drove the last ten miles through Sardine Canyon, Matthew began singing a song I had never heard before. "That's pretty," I said when he finished. "What's it called?"

" 'Truly Madly Deeply.' "

"Who sings it?"

"A group called Savage Garden."

"I've never heard of them."

"No, you wouldn't have," he said.

"What do you mean?"

He looked over and smiled. "They're an Australian group."

"Savage Garden," I said. "I'll look for them next time I go to a record store."

A peculiar grin spread across his face. "Let me know if you find them."

We arrived at the ranch after dark, but we'd made good time, arriving a full half-hour before our reservation at seven. Matthew pulled the car into a small, plowed lot near an illuminated visitors center.

"Here we are," he said. "The Hardware Ranch."

"Are you hungry?" I asked.

"In spite of eating almost all of your granola, I am. What's in the picnic basket?"

I reached in back. "I made my *not famous*, but still very good, chicken salad pitas." I pulled one out of the basket and handed it to him. "There you go. And I brought hot cocoa to drink. Oh, and for dessert there's chocolate cake."

"Nice," he said. He unwrapped the cellophane from the pita and took a bite. "Should be famous," he said.

"Fame doesn't make it taste any better."

"No, it just confirms your suspicion that it's good."

We finished everything except the cake. At five minutes to the hour we walked in to the visitors center. We picked up our tickets, then walked out on the patio behind the building. The mountain air was biting cold, as the temperature had dropped to single digits.

A man wearing a felt cowboy hat with a rattlesnake-skin band, a sheepskin jacket, and leather chaps and gloves, was standing next to a long black wooden sleigh hitched to two huge Clydesdales. The sleigh had four benches inside and there were electric spotlights connected to the front of the sleigh.

"I'm Roger," he said with a western drawl. "I'll be your driver tonight. Welcome to the Hardware Ranch. We'll be riding over a few of our acres, not all of them," he said grinning, "as this is a moonlight ride, not a sunrise ride."

"The Hardware Ranch was originally a cattle ranch back in the early 1900s. But as people started moving into the valley, the natural feeding places for the elk began to disappear. So the State of Utah purchased the ranch in 1945 and turned it into a wildlife preserve. Each year we feed more than six hundred head of elk. At night you won't be able to see the herd as you would during the day, but I venture we'll see a few and you most certainly will smell them. I guarantee it."

We climbed aboard the sleigh with about five other couples and a family with two small boys, who sat on the front row to be close to the horses.

There were thick wool blankets folded on the bench seats, and Matthew and I unfolded one and pulled it over us. Roger said, "Giddup," and slapped the reins, and the sleigh jerked forward behind the powerful animals across a pristine, snow-covered meadow that rolled out ahead of us like a great, moonlit sea.

Throughout the ride, Roger pointed out wildlife and answered questions, most of them from the young boys or their parents, but his voice was like a conversation at another table at a restaurant. We weren't there for a tour. We were seated on the back row of the sleigh with another young couple who were cuddled up and leaning the opposite direction, leaving a space between us. "This is beautiful," Matthew said. "Look at the stars."

I leaned back to take them in. In the absence of city lights the stars were highly visible, crisp and bright, as if they'd been polished off and hung above us as part of the ride.

"Beautiful *and cold*," I said, my teeth starting to chatter.

He smiled. "Isn't that the idea?"

"Whatever do you mean?" I said playfully.

He put his arm around me, pulling me tightly into his warm, firm body. With his other hand, he grasped my arm beneath the blanket, slid his hand down to my hands, which were clasped in my lap, and held them. I lay my head on his shoulder and closed my eyes, disappearing into his warmth, the sound of the horses' gait, the smooth glide of the sleigh and the cold, wet air against my face. I felt so amazingly happy and secure—happier than I had felt in years.

For the rest of the ride neither of us spoke, and I wanted to believe that it was because words were too clumsy for what we were feeling. I wondered if Matthew was feeling the same thing and hoped he was.

About an hour after we'd started out, the lights of the distant visitors center came back into view. I sighed. "I don't want this to end," I said. I looked up into Matthew's eyes. "Ever."

He was gazing at me intensely but sadly. "Me too," he said. Then he said softly, "How can you love the stream and not love the source?"

I looked at him quizzically. "What?"

"Nothing." He reached his hand up from the blanket and drew a finger across my cheek, down my jaw then to my lips. Then he softly cupped my chin and pulled it forward slightly as he leaned forward and we kissed. If I had thought I was in paradise before, I was now sure of it, engrossed in a delicious buffet of irony: hard and soft, passionate and gentle, thrill and peace, femininity and masculinity. The kiss was everything I had hoped it would be when I first hoped it would be. When he leaned back, I honestly felt a little dizzy, the way you feel when an amusement park ride suddenly comes to an end.

Our sleigh slid into the gate behind the center and came

to an abrupt stop. Roger turned around. "I'd like to thank you all for joining us. Hope you had a pleasant evening and be sure to come back and see us again real soon."

"Come on," I said, grabbing Matthew's hand, "Let's go." We walked back to the car. Matthew opened my door but I shut it. "Let's get in back," I said. I opened the back door and climbed in, moved the picnic basket to the front seat, then reached my hand out to him. He just stood there looking slightly nervous.

"Come on," I said. He slightly nodded, then climbed in and shut the door behind himself. I leaned into him, pressing my body, then lips, against his. He didn't resist, but he wasn't all there either. After a minute I pulled back, hurt and a little angry. "What's wrong?"

He shook his head. "I'm sorry . . ."

"Why won't you kiss me? Aren't you attracted to me?"

He looked deeply into my eyes. "Of course I am. You're gorgeous." He sighed. "I'm sorry. I guess I'm just not ready for a physical relationship. I feel like I'm betraying her."

"Don't you think she wants you to be happy?"

He didn't answer. He looked more than sad; he looked tormented. My hurt went away, replaced with sympathy.

"I'm sorry. That wasn't fair. I guess this is new territory for me. My husband ran off with every woman he met and you're still loyal to your wife after she's gone." I looked into his eyes. "That's really beautiful. You have a beautiful soul. It's okay. I'll wait until you're ready, no matter how long it takes."

"Thank you."

"Would you be okay holding me?"

He nodded. "I'd like that."

I turned around and lay back into him. He wrapped his strong, warm arms around me. *I loved this man.* Truthfully, the anticipation only heightened my feelings for him.

"I didn't know there were men like you," I said.

He didn't say anything.

I reached up and caressed his head, my fingers sliding under his ears and back through his hair. "What is it about you? There's something about you that I just can't put my finger on. Something . . ." I shook my head. "I don't know, just curious."

"Curious?"

"Like when I asked you what year you graduated from school, you had to think about it. Or how you diagnosed Charlotte without even seeing her. What is it about you that you're not telling me?"

"What do you think I'm hiding?"

"I have no idea. Who are you, Mr. Matthew?"

"Now there's a question." He pulled me in tighter. "Trust me, you really don't want to know."

CHAPTER

Twenty-three

I call it the Cardall Principle: The chance of finding a Band-Aid in your soup is directly proportionate to how much you're enjoying it.

✦ Beth Cardall's Diary ✦

When I think back to that time, my life should have been bliss. Charlotte was healthy again, and I had fallen in love with a sweet, beautiful man who loved both me and my daughter. It *should* have been perfect. But, as Roxanne always said, "Every rose has its thorns."

The first of the thorns arrived in the mailbox the following Thursday. I had just gotten home from work and was going though the mail when I came across a letter from my mortgage company. It was a final late-payment warning. I had ten days to bring my payments up to date or the bank would start foreclosure proceedings.

I was terrified. I had no money. Marc's life insurance was long gone, as was my emergency stash. Marc and I had never been late paying bills, but now, with only one paycheck, and a meager one at that, I was on a sinking ship. I went to my room and cried.

Matthew came over that evening around six. He walked in carrying a white plastic sack. "Look what I found," he said

excitedly. "Gluten-free bread. It's made from rice flour." He handed me the sack.

"Thank you," I said, my voice still weak from crying.

His smile fell. "What's wrong?"

I wiped at my eyes as I carried the bread to the kitchen. "Nothing."

"Something's obviously wrong. You can tell me."

I turned to look at him. "I'm just upset. I got a letter from my bank."

His brow furrowed. "What kind of letter?"

I retrieved the letter from the counter and handed it to him. He looked it over, then set it down without saying anything.

"It's just so embarrassing," I said. "I feel like a criminal or something."

"How much do you need?"

"I'm not taking your money."

"How about a loan, just enough to catch up."

"It doesn't matter. I still couldn't pay you back." I started to cry. "I just keep falling further behind. I just don't make enough."

He walked around the counter and put his arms around me. I laid my head on his shoulder. "The house is too big for us anyway. We don't need all this."

"I'm sorry," he said. He thought for a minute then asked, "How much equity do you have in your home?"

I sniffed. "I don't know. I owe sixty-eight thousand dollars. I don't know what it's worth. Maybe a hundred twenty thousand."

"I think you could get a lot more if you made a few improvements."

"I can't afford that, I have no money. That would only get me in more debt."

"You won't need much. And I'll do the work for free."

I looked up at him. "You can do carpentry?"

"My father was a home builder. I grew up working weekends remodeling homes."

"You would do that for me?"

"Of course," he said matter-of-factly. "It would be a shame to let this house go for only a hundred twenty thousand. So here's the plan. First, you don't want to sell a house in winter. There are fewer buyers and it will show a lot better in spring. So you take out a home-equity loan, enough to catch up on the payments and a few thousand extra to make some improvements, then, in April we sell your home. I think you could get an extra forty or fifty thousand out of it. That's a lot of hours at the dry cleaner."

"You would really do that for me?"

He touched my cheek. "Of course."

I threw my arms around him. "Why are you so good to me?"

He smiled. "Because I like you."

That evening we walked around the house with a clipboard, paper and pen. We decided that the main floor only needed a little touch-up on the baseboards, a new shower curtain and tile in the master bathroom. The basement had been roughed in but was basically unfinished, needing drywall, carpet and paint. There were a few repairs outside the house as well: a shutter needed to be fixed and the north-side rain gutter needed replacing.

After we had surveyed the house, we sat down at the kitchen table with the list. "I can do everything downstairs except the carpet," Matthew said, tapping a pencil on the notepad as he thought through the work. "Drywall isn't expensive. I'm guessing around four thousand, maybe five, depending on the quality of the carpet. I bet I could find a wholesaler and an independent carpet layer. I'd plan on about five, tops. With the extra finished rooms I'm betting you could sell for around a hundred fifty to a hundred sixty thousand."

"That would solve my financial problems."

"For a while," he said. "And in the meantime, you wouldn't have to worry about finding a new place right now and moving in winter."

I walked over and sat on his lap, draping my arms around his neck. I kissed his cheek, then lay my head on his shoulder. "I can't believe how lucky I am to have you. I love you."

He was quiet a moment, then said, "I love you too." After a few more minutes he exhaled deeply. "I'd better go."

"Do you have to?"

"Sorry. I've got some things I need to do in the morning."

"If you must," I pouted. I got off his lap and walked him to the door.

"Can you take some time off at lunch tomorrow?" he asked.

I nodded. "Sure."

"We need to open up that home-equity loan, so I can get started."

"Oh," I said. "I thought you were offering to take me out to lunch."

He touched my cheek and his smile returned. "I'll do that too." He looked into my face. "You know, you're too beautiful for your own good. Or at least mine."

"You make me feel beautiful," I said.

He kissed me on the cheek. "Good night, Beth."

"Good night. Sweet dreams. I'll see you tomorrow."

He stepped back from me, then walked outside. I stood at the open door, shutting it only after he drove away. "Girl, you are in way over your head," I said to myself. "Way, way over your head." I smiled, then went to bed.

CHAPTER

Twenty-four

If I were queen of the world, there wouldn't be money.

✦ Beth Cardall's Diary ✦

The next morning was overcast, with sporadic snow flurries. I was back at the press when Teresa walked by. She was wearing a leotard body suit that accentuated her curves.

"Hey, Beth, have you been lifting weights?"

I looked at her quizzically. "No. Why?"

"I don't know, you just look different. Prettier." Her observation sounded more like a complaint than a compliment. "My boyfriend noticed," she said, and walked off.

I couldn't help but smile. The truth was, I *felt* prettier. An hour later I told Roxanne about the exchange.

"It's true, baby doll. I've never seen you this gorgeous. Never. And you have always been beautiful."

"He makes me feel beautiful. He makes me so happy."

She smiled. "Happy is pretty too."

Matthew came by the cleaners to pick me up a little after noon. As usual, he came in through the front lobby. As I walked from the back to greet him, Teresa walked around the front counter. "Hi, handsome."

I stopped when I saw her approach him. Roxanne was in back ironing vests and was watching as well. "What is she doing?" Suddenly she turned red. "She's hitting on your man. I'm going to kill that little hussy," she said, setting down the iron. "I'm going to stick her head in a buck press."

"Wait," I said. "I want to see this."

Teresa moved seductively toward him. "Can I help you?"

Matthew looked amused. "You must be Teresa."

She smiled coquettishly. "How did you know?"

"Your reputation precedes you. Would you mind telling Beth I'm here?"

Her smile fell. "Sure." She walked back, surprised to find both Roxanne and I standing there. Roxanne glared at her but held her tongue.

"Your man's here," she said snidely.

"Thank you, Teresa," I said.

"Don't mention it. I'm going to the bathroom." She stormed off.

"Revenge is sweet," Roxanne said. "Like nectar."

"See you, hon," I said.

"Have a good lunch."

Matthew smiled when he saw me. He greeted me with a hug. "Ready?"

"Ready."

When we were in his car, I said, "So you met Teresa."

"Yeah. Was she hitting on me?"

"Yes."

"Doesn't she know I'm yours?"

The way he said that made me happy on many levels. "She knew."

"What a skank," he said.

I burst out laughing. "I just love you."

✦

Outside of shopping, I pretty much hate anything to do with money, and the visit to the bank was even more excruciating than I thought it would be. I didn't understand all the talk about points, HELOCs and adjustable rates. In the end, all I came away with was that I was approved for a $63,000 loan.

As we were finishing the paperwork, Matthew asked, "Do you mind if we make me a cosignatory on the loan? That way you won't have to come down here every time I need to buy supplies."

"Fine with me," I said. "I hate this stuff." I looked at the loan officer. "No offense to you."

"None taken," he said. "You'll just need to sign here."

I signed my name on the line he pointed to.

Matthew asked, "How much do you need to catch up your mortgage?"

"Let's see. It's nine hundred thirty-seven dollars a month, and I'm two months behind."

"Almost nineteen hundred. Let's take out twenty-eight hundred right now. That will cover you until April when we list the house."

"That sounds good," I said.

"Make the check out to Beth Cardall," Matthew said.

"I'll be just a minute," the banker said, rising.

I said to Matthew, "Thank you for helping me."

He smiled. "My pleasure," he said.

For the first time in weeks the gnawing pain of debt was gone.

We walked out of the bank with a folder full of documents. "This belongs to you," Matthew said, handing me the packet. "Now where would you like to go to lunch?"

"On a day like this, soup sounds kind of good."

"There's a great little soup place by my apartment. They have the best split-pea soup."

"I hate split-pea."

"That's not all they have," he said. "It's just what I like."

The restaurant was not what I expected. It was a small, cluttered dive, though surprisingly popular. I held a table for us while Matthew got our soup—split-pea for him, tomato basil for me—with Diet Cokes and a turkey sandwich to share.

As we were eating, I said, "You said you live around here."

Matthew nodded. "Just over on the next street."

"Can I see where you live?"

He looked a little uncomfortable. "It's not much to look at. It's a basement apartment. I moved here without a place to stay so I just took the first place I found."

"Could we at least drive by?"

"If we must," he said.

After we finished eating, we climbed into his car and

drove by his apartment. I understood why he was hesitant to show me his place. The neighborhood was poor. The homes were unkempt and overgrown and the yards filled with clutter. The house where Matthew rented was old and decrepit, with a broken-down truck in the side yard next to a large stack of rusted pipes. The entry to his apartment was on the side of the house and was entered by a flight of concrete steps covered by a corrugated plastic roof. His BMW looked remarkably out of place in the neighborhood. I was surprised that he would live in such a run-down place.

"I warned you," he said.

"It's not so bad," I replied.

"Are you crazy?" he said smiling. "It's a dump. This place makes the landfill look like Central Park."

"You're right, it's awful. Aren't you afraid to park your car here?"

"A little. Now you know why we meet at your place. But don't worry. I'm going to be moving soon. I'm about to close a big deal."

"You're working again?"

"I never really stopped. I've always got my fingers in a few deals. This is the big one I've been waiting for."

"Sounds exciting."

"Believe me, it's a big one. Best of all, it's a sure bet."

I had no idea that his sure bet somehow involved me.

CHAPTER

Twenty-five

Only fools and children believe that covering your eyes makes the monsters go away.

✦ Beth Cardall's Diary ✦

It snowed through the night, enough to bring out the snow-plows, and I woke to the sound of a plow's metal blade scraping down our street. As much as I wanted to sleep in, I got up and dressed. Then I got Charlotte dressed and ready for the day.

In light of my financial crisis I had asked Roxanne to schedule me on Saturdays to bring in a little extra cash. My neighbor, Margaret, offered to save me child-care expenses by inviting Charlotte over to play with Katie for the day.

Even though Prompt didn't clean or press clothing on weekends, Saturday mornings were still the busiest day of the week with pickups and drop-offs. Predictably we were swamped, and our small lobby was crowded to capacity, with more customers waiting outside the doors, their arms full of clothing. I was busy ringing up an order when Roxanne answered the phone. She shouted to me over the din. "Beth, it's your neighbor."

"She's got Charlotte. Tell her I'll be right there." I hurriedly finished the transaction I was working on, then grabbed the phone from the counter. "Margaret?"

"Hi, Beth. I hope I didn't catch you at a bad time." Her voice was tense.

"Is Charlotte all right?"

"She's fine. She and Katie are in the backyard making a snowman. I called for another reason. My husband George just called from work. Did you know he works at Zions Bank?"

I wondered what this could possibly have to do with me and if it could wait. "No, I didn't."

"He's the manager at the Holladay Branch. A transaction came across his desk yesterday afternoon that he's a little concerned about."

"A transaction?"

"It's in your name. How well do you know Matthew Principato?"

The way she asked made me nervous. "Pretty well. Why?"

"I don't mean to alarm you, I'm sure there's a reasonable explanation, I just felt I should check with you to be sure. Did you know that Matthew took a loan out against your house?"

I breathed out in relief. "Oh, yes. I know. He's helping me make some home improvements, so I put him on the account so he could take money out when he needed it."

"That's what George said. I know this is very personal, but do you mind me asking how much he was supposed to take out?"

"Well, I think he said it would be about three or four thousand dollars. And we took some out at the bank as well. But he wasn't going to take it all at once."

"Oh, no," Margaret said.

"Is there a problem?"

"Beth, he's taken a lot more than that."

"How much more?"

"He took more than sixty thousand."

My chest constricted. "What?"

"George said he maxed out the home-equity loan."

"Why didn't he stop him?"

"I'm sorry. George didn't handle the transaction, but he said it was perfectly legal, Matthew was on the account."

I felt as if someone had just slugged me in the gut. "I've got to go."

Margaret sensed my panic. "I'm sorry. Maybe there's an explanation."

"I'm sure there is," I said angrily. "He wanted my money. Thank you for calling."

As I hung up the phone, Roxanne stared at me. "Hey, what's wrong, hon? What happened?"

I just looked at her, breathless.

"Teresa," Roxanne said. "Cover for us."

Teresa looked at her incredulously. "There's like, a million people."

"Deal with it." Roxanne walked me back to the break room. She pulled a chair out at the table and sat me in it. That's when I completely melted down.

"Honey, tell me what happened. Is it Matthew?"

"What have I done?"

"He broke up with you?"

I wiped my face. "He stole my home."

"What?"

"It was a setup. He never loved me. He was playing me all along."

"I don't believe that. Tell me what happened."

"He offered to remodel my basement, so yesterday we set up a loan and I gave him access to my account so he could take money out for materials. He took every penny. Sixty-three thousand dollars." I almost hyperventilated saying it.

Roxanne gasped. "Oh, honey."

"I'm such an idiot. He's one of those guys you read about who preys on desperate, gullible women. He steals their life savings, then disappears. How could I have been so stupid?"

"How could you know? We were all enchanted by him. Anyone could have made that mistake. Can you find him?"

"I know where he lives."

"Go. Teresa and I will cover for you. I'll call Jan and have her pick up Charlotte. She can spend the night at our place."

"Thank you." I leaned into Roxanne and broke down again. She patted my back. "There, there, honey. Maybe it's not what it seems."

"What else could it be?"

She groaned. "Oh, baby."

"I wanted it to be good. I wanted to be loved by someone."

"It's my fault," Roxanne said, "I wanted it for you. I pushed you into it."

"It's not your fault. It's what I really wanted. I wanted it so bad I closed my eyes."

I was nearly hysterical and blind with tears as I drove from the cleaners to his apartment. I was fortunate that chance had taken me there just a few days earlier, as up to that point I had no way to contact him. My mind replayed our last conversation. Is this what he meant by the "big deal—sure thing" he was about to close? He had played me like a Stradivarius.

I parked my car in front of his house, sliding the front of my car into a bank of snow, and climbed out. I looked for his car but, not surprisingly, it wasn't there. It had snowed through the night and the cement walkway to his apartment had not been shoveled. I could see footprints coming out of it.

I followed them down the stairs to his apartment. There was no doorbell so I pounded on the door. "Matthew! Open up." I pounded again, then checked the doorknob and found it was unlocked. I pushed open the door. Through the dim light from the window wells I couldn't believe what I saw.

The room was empty. The only furniture was a twin mattress on the floor in the corner of the room with a sofa pillow and a wool blanket.

"Matthew!" I screamed. I turned on the light, a single, naked globe above the kitchen sink, and walked through the house.

In the bathroom there was a can of cheap shaving cream and a disposable razor on the tile counter, next to a bottle of Old Spice, a bar of soap and a tube of Prell shampoo. I went into his bedroom. There was no furniture, just two cardboard boxes—one was empty and the other had some white briefs and two pairs of socks. I opened the closet. Inside, on a hanger, was only one shirt, the red flannel shirt he had worn on our date to the ranch and likely abandoned. I went back out to the kitchen. The fridge held a nearly empty plastic gallon jug of milk, two cans of Coke and a salami sandwich that had mold growing on one side. The cupboards were bare except for a box of Grape-Nuts and Cap'n Crunch cereal.

There was a full plastic garbage can next to the stove. I dumped it out on the kitchen floor. The contents were mostly fast-food wrappers and empty soda cans. I combed through it hoping to find something that might give me a clue to where he'd gone. I came across a folded scrap of paper, scrawled in ink were the words "U of U, Beta. Todd Fey, 292-9145. Fake I.D."

I gasped. I didn't even know his real name. I shoved the note into my pants pocket and kicked the wall on the way out of his apartment.

I went upstairs to the house's front door and rang the bell. It was a couple of minutes before the door opened to an old man. He was short, with a ragged gray beard, and he looked at me with an expression of annoyance. "No solicitors," he growled.

"I'm looking for the man who rents from you downstairs."

"I don't know anything about him." He started to close the door.

"Wait," I said, pushing against the door. "He stole from me. You can tell me or I'll call the police and you can talk to them."

He scowled but seemed frightened by my threat. "What do you want?"

"Did you see him leave this morning?"

"Didn't see nothing."

"Do you have an address for him?"

He looked at me as if I was stupid. "*This* is his address."

"I mean, maybe there was a different one on a check, when he paid his rent."

"He always paid in cash. That's all I know. He stole from you? You call the police. He always paid his rent, that's all I know." He shut the door and locked it.

I stepped down from the porch as tears welled up in my eyes. I drove to the Conoco gas station on the corner across from the soup restaurant where we'd eaten a few days earlier. I foraged through my car for a quarter, then went to the pay phone. I took the note I'd found out of my pocket and dialed the number.

A young voice answered. "Beta Sigma Pi, Delta Eta chapter, this is Pledge David speaking."

"I'm looking for Todd Fey."

"Just a moment." I heard him shout, "Is Todd here?" I heard a few grunts, then after what seemed an eternity a different voice answered.

"This is Todd."

"My name is Beth Cardall. I found your name on a paper. You made a fake I.D. for Matthew Principato."

"I don't know what you're talking about," he said nervously.

"I'm not trying to get you in trouble or anything. I'm looking for this man. He stole from me."

"You got the wrong guy." He hung up.

Smart, I thought. *Real smart.*

I got back in my car and drove the gray, slushy streets around Holladay, Cottonwood Heights, and Murray for nearly five hours looking for his car. At one point I followed a navy BMW for nearly ten minutes until the driver pulled into a gas station and I saw that the driver was an elderly woman. I finally went home around nine. I called and checked on Charlotte.

"What did you find?" Roxanne asked.

"His apartment was abandoned," I said. "And I found a phone number where he got his fake I.D."

"Holy mother-of-pearl," she said. "Have you called the police?"

"What could they do? Everything he did was legal."

"Oh, baby. What are you going to do?"

"I'm going out looking again in the morning. Is Charlotte okay?"

"Yes. She's asleep. Don't worry about a thing, we'll take care of her."

"Thank you." I started to cry. "I can't believe this is happening. What did I do to deserve all this?"

"You don't deserve any of this. I don't know why bad

things happen to good people, but don't you believe for a second you did anything to bring this on yourself."

"But I did, Rox. I totally brought this on myself."

"Don't say that. What did you do to bring this on your-self?"

"I trusted."

CHAPTER

Twenty-six

The most dangerous of all indulgences is trust.

✦ Beth Cardall's Diary ✦

Sunday morning was gray, the sky streaked with dark, spidery clouds. I got up early and went out looking again—still wearing the same clothes from the day before. Nothing. It was around five in the afternoon that I faced the inevitable. He was gone. My money was gone. My house was gone. He had probably skipped town, gone back to Italy or wherever it was he really came from. I pulled into a Kmart parking lot and called Roxanne from a pay phone.

"Any luck?" she asked.

"No," I said crying. "He's vanished."

"I was hoping you'd call. I've got *news*."

"What?"

"This morning I told Ray about what had happened, and he said that he saw Matthew yesterday afternoon at the Chevron station. I asked him how he knew who Matthew was and he said he didn't, that Matthew had just walked up to him and asked if he was my husband."

"How he know that?"

"I have no idea. Anyway, Ray didn't know he had stolen your money, so they were just slinging spit, you know, talking man stuff. Ray asked if he was going to watch the Mike Tyson fight, and Matthew said he was headed to Wendover to put a little down on it."

"Oh, no," I said.

Wendover is a small gambling town about an hour and a half from Salt Lake City just over the Nevada border—a cultural by-product of Utah's antigambling laws.

"I've got to go out there," I said. "I'm going to get my money back."

"Honey, let me and Ray go with you."

"No. I'm going to do this. I have to do this."

"Honey, you be careful. There's no telling what he might be capable of."

I ran back out to my car. So that was it. *He was a gambler.* A thief, a liar and a gambler, and he was about to lose Charlotte's and my future.

The drive to Wendover is 120 miles west on I-80, passing the Great Salt Lake and the Bonneville Salt Flats, one of the flattest places on the planet—so flat that you can see the curvature of the earth. The flats are the grounds where dozens of world land speed records were claimed, from Ab Jenkins's 1935 Duesenberg "Mormon Meteor" to Craig Breedlove's "Spirit of America," the first car to reach 600 mph.

For me it was a hundred miles of nothing to see—nothing to distract me from the cauldron of panic that boiled in my chest. I wondered how many other women Matthew (I could barely think his name without feeling sick) had scammed in this way.

On a practical basis there were other things to worry

about. *What would happen when I got there? Would I find him? Was he violent? Would the casino help me? What if he had already lost all my money?*

First Marc and now Matthew. I wondered why I was so adept at attracting broken men. Maybe they were all broken.

I reached the neon glow of Wendover around eight-thirty and drove past a sixty-four-foot-tall sheet-metal cowboy pointing down at the stripe across the road that separates Utah from Nevada. I stopped at the first casino I reached, the Rainbow Casino, a brightly lit trap in the desert landscape. I parked my car in the crowded parking lot and ran inside, fueled equally by adrenaline and emotion.

The casino interior was cavernous and crowded, echoing with the clinking, whirring sounds of slot machines and the electric song of illuminated wheels of fortune. I ran up to a tall, uniform-wearing man standing at the concierge desk.

"May I help you?" he asked.

"Where do they gamble on boxing?"

"The Tyson-Douglas fight," he said. He pointed past a large, illuminated field of slot machines. "Over past the lobby at the Race Book. But you're too late to get anything down, the fight's started."

"Am I too late to get my money back?"

He looked at me dully. "Once the fight starts, no money changes hands."

I stepped away from him, speechless. I was too late. I walked over to the part of the casino where the man had pointed. There was a large neon sign that read RACE AND SPORTSBOOK. Beneath the sign was a large bank of televisions—an entire wall of screens—the majority of them tuned to the boxing match. The Tyson-Douglas fight was clearly the main event, and a large, excited crowd of mostly men were talking and drinking and shouting out as the two fighters danced around the ring exchanging blows.

Then I saw him. Unlike the rest of the crowd, Matthew seemed detached from the event, sitting alone at a small round table. He held a drink in one hand. The sight of him made me feel sick and scared and angry in equal parts. "Matthew!" I shouted. He didn't respond. I shouted louder. "Matthew!"

He looked around, then over at me, clearly surprised to see me. He stood as I approached. "Beth. What are you doing here?"

"I want my money back."

He said calmly, "You'll get it. And a lot more."

"I want it *now*." Several of the other patrons looked over at us. "Hand it over," I shouted. "Now!"

He looked around, embarrassed by the attention I'd drawn. "I can't do that. I don't have it anymore."

"Who has it?"

"The casino."

"How much of it did you gamble?"

He looked at me warily. "Listen—"

"How much?!"

"All of it."

I slapped him. "You crook. That was everything we had." I began to hyperventilate. "That was Charlotte's schooling. That's what keeps us off the street. I can't believe I trusted you."

More people were now watching us than the monitors.

"Beth, you have to trust me. I would never do anything to hurt you."

I was crying. "Are you insane? You've hurt me more than anyone I've ever known. You've hurt me more than Marc."

"Beth, you don't understand." He reached out to me and I screamed.

"Don't you dare touch me! Don't you ever touch me again. I don't ever want to see you again." I began backing away from him. I was hysterical. "You stay away from me and my daughter. If I ever see you again, I'll call the police. Stay away from me!" I turned and ran out of the casino.

I sobbed almost the entire way home. I wanted to throw up. I wanted to drive my car across the divider into every semi I passed, and if it weren't for Charlotte, I might have. About thirty minutes from Salt Lake, just west of Tooele, I got pulled over by the highway patrol. I almost couldn't stop crying long enough to give the police officer my information.

The officer didn't give me a ticket. When I was finally able to tell him what Matthew had done, he was sympathetic. "Are you sure you can make it home?"

"Yes."

"I know you're upset, but slow down and drive carefully. We don't want to add an accident to this."

"Thank you, officer."

"You're welcome, ma'am." He handed me back my license. "You say it was the Tyson fight?"

I nodded. "Yes."

"Well, let's hope he bet on the long shot, because Tyson just got knocked out."

✦

I got home around midnight. Charlotte was still at Roxanne's, leaving the place as dark and empty as I felt inside. It had snowed off and on all day and my home was covered with nearly a foot of new snow. *My home?* It wasn't mine anymore. How could I have so casually lost it? How could I be so gullible? When he asked to be a cosignatory, his accessing my entire account had never even crossed my mind.

I think I cried all night. I cried less about the money than the confirmed reality that my deepest suspicions were right—he never wanted me. I was nothing to him but a dope. I was unlovable.

The next day I was still lying in bed at one in the afternoon when Jan brought Charlotte home.

"Mrs. C?" she shouted. "We're back."

I didn't want Jan or Charlotte to see me as I was, unshowered, undressed, my face puffy and tear-streaked. "Thank you, Jan," I said gruffly from behind the door. "Can I pay you tomorrow?"

"No problem, Mrs. C., Charlotte, Molly and I had a great time, didn't we, girl?"

"Yep."

"I'll see you later," I heard Jan say. "Give me skin."

A moment later my door opened. My bedroom was a cave, the blinds drawn and the light off. "Hi, Mom," Charlotte said. Through the darkness I could see she was holding her Molly doll and wearing an oversized raccoon-tail hat.

My voice was strained and weak, but I tried to sound normal. "Did you have a good time, honey?"

"Yep. Can I turn on the light?"

"Let's just leave it off."

"Are you sick?"

"I have a headache," I said.

She walked to my side, close enough to see that I had been crying. "What's wrong, Mom?"

"Nothing." Charlotte just stared at me. She knew better. "*Nothing* I can talk about."

"Is it Mr. Matthew?"

I burst into tears. *How could a six-year-old be so astute?* Charlotte climbed into bed and snuggled up with me. "You can hold Molly."

"Thank you. I'd rather hold you."

"Mr. Matthew said he wouldn't make you cry."

I ran my hands back over her cheeks, pulling back her long, blond hair. "He's not who we thought he was."

"He's not Mr. Matthew?"

"I don't know."

"Is he someone bad?"

"Yes, honey. He is."

"He didn't seem bad."

"People aren't always what they seem to be."

I didn't climb out of bed until five. I felt like I'd been run over by a motorcycle gang. Charlotte was at the kitchen table drawing pictures with crayon. I went to the kitchen to make her some dinner. I had just put some water on to boil when the doorbell rang. I wasn't expecting anybody and I didn't want to see anybody. "Charlotte, will you get that?"

"Sure, Mom." She put down her crayons and ran to the door.

I heard the door open, then after a moment I heard Charlotte say, "She's crying."

A minute later she walked back into the kitchen. "Mr. Matthew's here."

I looked at her in disbelief. "Matthew?"

She nodded.

I took the pan off the burner and turned off the stove. My heart filled with rage. It was something I had become good at—concealing heartbreak with anger.

Charlotte had left the front door open and as I walked into the foyer I saw him. He stood there, a few feet from the door wearing only a hooded sweatshirt, his arms wrapped around himself from the cold. He looked at me anxiously. I noticed he held something in his hand. An envelope.

"I told you I never wanted to see you again," I said fiercely.

"Here's your money back," he said, holding out the envelope. "It's all there with your winnings."

In spite of my anger I felt a tremendous flood of relief. I started to cry.

He said, "I'm sorry that you think I was trying to take advantage of you. I wasn't. I just didn't want you to lose your home."

I stood there glaring at him. "I don't want your *winnings*. I don't gamble."

"Neither do I."

"Then what do you call it?"

"It's not gambling if you already know how it ends." He pushed the envelope forward. "Take it."

I took the envelope without looking at it. "This doesn't change anything."

"You should open it."

The envelope wasn't sealed. I reached in and extracted a check from the envelope. It took a moment for the amount to register. I had never seen that many zeros on a check. I raised my hand to my face.

"Mike Tyson was a forty-two-to-one favorite," he said.

I couldn't speak.

"Beth, you have to trust me that I wouldn't do anything to hurt you. Ever. I went to Wendover for you. I only had your best interest in mind." He put his hands in his pockets.

"I never want to see you again," I said.

He looked stricken but not surprised. "If that's what you want." He pulled his hood up and turned and walked out to his car. I watched him drive away. He never looked back.

Charlotte walked up as I shut the door. "Is he still bad?"

Still clutching the check I crouched down and hugged her. "I don't know what he is."

CHAPTER

Twenty-seven

I don't know what to think. Matthew didn't just upset the game board, he changed the pieces, the dice and the rules. Actually he changed the whole game board too.

✦ Beth Cardall's Diary ✦

The next morning at work Roxanne just stared at the check. "Holy moly, holy moly, holy moly. Is this real?"

"It's a money order."

"Two million six hundred and four thousand dollars. You're quitting, right?"

"I have no idea what I'm going to do. This is overwhelming."

"He really gave it all to you. Every penny."

I nodded. "I think so."

"I tell you, the man is an angel. And if he wasn't before, he just earned his wings."

"He's not an angel," I said. "He deceived me. I can't trust him."

Roxanne gave me her sternest gaze. "Girl, did someone beat you with a stupid stick? How much more trustworthy could he be? He could have taken all that money and never looked back. But he didn't. *He gave it all to you.*" She held up the check. "You got two million dollars' worth of trustworthy right here. What more proof could anyone ask for?"

I thought over her words. "You think I made a mistake?"

"A mistake? No. Fighting a land war in Asia is a mistake. What you did was epic stupidity. Tossing out the best man you've ever known. Criminee, the best man I've ever known. You should be worshiping the water he walks on."

I exhaled. "I'm such an idiot."

"This time I'm not disagreeing, girl. You go find him and beg him to take you back."

"What if he's gone?"

"Then I'd search every inch of pavement in this city until I found him."

I took a deep breath. "It's okay if I leave?"

"I'll fire you if you don't."

I kissed her cheek. "Thanks, Rox."

"Yeah, you better thank me." I heard her grumbling after me. "God must love fools 'cause he sure made a lot of them."

CHAPTER

Twenty-eight

*Clearly, there is more to heaven and Utah
than is dreamt of in my philosophy.*

✦ Beth Cardall's Diary ✦

Matthew's car wasn't at his apartment, so I drove around the area looking for him. Around six o'clock I was driving back to his place to check again when I noticed his BMW, or at least one like it, parked at a sports bar just down the street from his apartment. I parked next to it and looked inside the car. I recognized his coat.

I walked inside the building and spotted him sitting alone in the corner sipping a drink. I took a deep breath, then walked up to him. "Hi."

He looked up at me but didn't smile. *"Ciao."*

"I've been looking everywhere for you."

"You said you never wanted to see me again."

"Yeah, I did, didn't I. May I join you?" He looked at me sadly, then gestured to the chair across from him. I pulled off my coat and sat down. "I'm very sorry."

"So two million dollars can buy remorse?"

His words stung. "It's not the money. I mean, it was. I was afraid I'd lost it all, but I was also afraid . . ." I hesitated. "That you didn't really love me."

"How could you doubt me?"

"After Marc, can you blame me for doubting?"

He took another drink, then looked at me. "No, I guess not. But you were right, the best thing would be for me to just go away and never come back."

I stared at him, my eyes welling up in tears. "No, that wouldn't be best. Please, give me another chance. I know I screwed up. But I'll make it up to you. I promise."

"It's not that, Beth."

I looked at him, confused. "Then what is it?"

He stared at his drink for a moment then said, "You don't really know who I am."

"It doesn't matter to me who you are. What I know of you is enough. I don't even care if your name isn't Matthew. I don't care about your past. All I want is your future."

"My name *is* Matthew," he said softly. "But that's the thing—my past *does* matter and my future is spoken for. In a way, they're the same thing."

"What do you mean?"

He looked down for a long time. "You wouldn't believe me if I told you."

"Believe what?" I touched his hand. "Matthew, I'll believe you. Trust me."

"You really want to know who I am?"

"I do."

He groaned. "I'm a mistake, Beth. I'm a big, freaking cosmic mistake." He rubbed his face. "I was never supposed to fall in love with you."

"How can falling in love be a mistake?"

"Trust me, it can." He rubbed his chin. His voice lowered. "You have no idea what's really happening here. The best thing I could do for everyone is walk away and never come back. Especially for Charlotte."

"Charlotte loves you."

"Exactly." He looked me in the eyes. "Beth, there are forces at work here you couldn't possibly understand."

My brow furrowed. "What kind of forces?"

"I honestly don't know." He looked at me for a long time, then I saw his demeanor relax in resignation. "All right, you want to know? Here you go. I told you that I don't gamble. I don't. I knew about the boxing match because I watched it."

"A lot of people watched it."

"I watched it *eighteen years ago.*"

"What?"

"Beth, this isn't my time. I'm supposed to be ten years old, not twenty-seven." He stared into my eyes then said flatly, "I came here from the future."

"The future?"

"Two thousand eight, to be exact."

For a moment I just stared at him, wondering what had gotten into him. "Why are you saying this?"

He shook his head. "I told you you wouldn't believe me." He lifted a glass and took a drink, his eyes never leaving me. "I'm not lying. How else would I know about the boxing match?"

"It could have been a lucky guess."

"It could have been," he said nodding, "but not likely. How did I know that Charlotte had celiac disease even though I had never seen her and all the doctors who examined her couldn't diagnose her?"

"I don't know."

"How did I know that your real name is Bethany—Bethany Ann Curtis, or that you like sunflowers instead of roses or what you eat at your favorite restaurant?"

I just stared at him. I had no idea.

"How about this—you were born in Magna, Utah, and your father, Charles Donald Curtis, a volunteer fireman, left you when you were six. Your mother, Donna, is buried in Elysian Gardens and every Memorial Day you go to her grave and lay a lavender plant."

"How are you doing this?"

"I'm not making this up, Beth. I'm not even good at this. I kept slipping up, like in the car when I said how much I like your granola when you'd never made it before. Or when you asked me what year I had graduated, what was I going to say? In nine more years? I told Jan that I had heard a lot about her even though you had never mentioned her. Do you want to know her future? I know her as Jan Klaus, a married women. She gets a big tattoo on her arm, marries a veterinarian and moves to Portland, where she has a boy named Ethan. She calls Charlotte almost every month."

Just then the waitress came to our table. "Do you need anything else?"

"No, thank you," Matthew said. He handed her a bill. "Keep the change."

When she was gone, he continued. "I hadn't heard of the Bee Gees, not because I was in Italy, but because I hadn't been born yet. That song I was singing to you in the canyon, 'Truly Madly Deeply,' hasn't been written yet. There is no

Savage Garden group. That's why I smiled when you said you were going to look for it.

"I can tell you every U.S. president for the next twenty years. I can tell you most of the Oscar best-picture winners, every Super Bowl winner. Every World Series winner. I can even tell you almost every *American Idol* winner."

"What's *American Idol*?"

"It's a TV show. And in twelve years you're going to be a big fan. The point is, I know the future because I've been there. I can tell you about world events. A year from now a war will start in Kuwait."

"Kuwait?"

"It's a little country in the Middle East with a lot of oil. Later this year they'll be invaded by Iraq and next year the U.S. will go to war to liberate them. Operation Desert Shield. Of course the biggest news is that the Soviet Union falls apart."

"That's impossible."

"Yeah, well so is Mike Tyson getting knocked out by a forty-two-to-one underdog. If history teaches us anything, it's that anything is possible and the unlikely is likely. The changes I told you about have already begun."

I looked down, struggling to process all he was saying.

"I know about your husband, Marc, and that you never told Charlotte that he cheated. I also know that he gave you a pearl necklace that you won't wear. I'm guessing that's because it was a sin offering."

"How did you know that?"

"Because Charlotte knows it's in your closet drawer and

has always wondered why you wouldn't wear it. I know that on the eve of Charlotte's birthdays you come in at night after you think she's sleeping and tell her how lucky you are that she came into your life and then you say goodbye to your baby girl."

"Stop it," I said.

"When Charlotte gets married, you give her the rose-gold locket that your mother gave you."

I yelled, "Stop it!" I began to cry. "How are you doing this?"

He grabbed my arm. "I told you. I'm from your future. I can tell you things you don't want to know. The dry cleaner burns down in six years. One of the workers, Bill or Phil, or whatever his name is, dies of a heart attack. Roxanne's husband has a stroke."

"Ray?"

He stared at me. "You don't want to know what I know. I've already told you too much."

I felt like I'd fallen down the rabbit hole. I lay my head in my hands. After a few moments I looked back up. "If you're from the future, why are you so interested in me? Why not save the world."

"Because it's not mine to save. The world has its own destiny. I wasn't sent here to change the world. Only yours."

"Someone sent you?"

"I don't know, some*one*, some*thing*. Who knows? Maybe it's some cosmic committee. I'm here because I made Charlotte a promise."

"You know Charlotte as an adult?"

He hesitated, his eyes carefully reading mine. "This is going to be hard for you."

"What?"

He took a deep breath. "Beth, Charlotte is my wife."

I stared at him. "What?"

He raked his hand back through his hair. "I made her a promise that I would take care of you."

"But you told me your wife died."

His expression turned grave. "I've told you too much."

"What happens to Charlotte?"

"Don't ask, Beth."

"Tell me."

After a moment he threw up his hands. "Nothing happens to Charlotte. Okay? Just forget all this. None of this is true. I'm just a lunatic you'll never have to see again."

"What happens to Charlotte?"

"Nothing."

I grabbed him. "I need to know."

"Some things are better not to know. You said so yourself."

"I was wrong."

He groaned and balanced his head on one hand, covering his eyes. A minute later he looked up. "She gets intestinal lymphoma from her celiac."

My eyes welled up. "I don't believe you. I don't know how you're doing this, but I don't believe you."

"Good," he almost shouted. "Don't."

When I could speak, I said, "You're my son-in-law?"

He didn't answer. "Supposing that what you've told me is true, how did you get here?"

He shook his head. "I have no idea. It was 2008, just three days before Christmas. Charlotte and I had been to the oncologist to discuss the results of her last round of chemo and radiation. We were hopeful that she was in remission, but we were dead wrong. The doctor said that the cancer had spread and that now we'd have to resort to unconventional methods.

"It was the worst day of my life. Charlotte collapsed at the doctor's office. I think it was the last straw. After all she'd been through, she finally just gave up. That afternoon you called to check on her and she made me lie to you. She didn't want to ruin your Christmas. But she stayed in bed after that.

"Then, on Christmas Eve, Charlotte and I were supposed to go to your house for a dinner party, but Charlotte couldn't get out of bed. She had me call to tell you that we wouldn't be making it but we'd see you in the morning for breakfast."

I began to cry.

"It was around eight that I climbed in bed next to her and started giving her a massage to help her sleep. I knew she was bad off, I just didn't want to believe how bad. She started talking about you. She said that you had lost everyone you had ever loved and that you had given your entire life for her. She was upset that she had let you down."

I dabbed my eyes with the napkin. "She never let me down."

"She said, 'When I'm gone, promise me that you'll take care of her.' I told her, 'You're not going anywhere,' but she shook her head. 'Please,' she said. 'Promise me.'

"I promised her I would, then she fell asleep. I just lay there next to her, terrified of losing her, wondering if I should call someone, praying for her life." He took a deep breath. "Wondering if it was time for her to die." He slowly shook his head. "That's the last thing I remember. That's the last time I saw her.

"The next thing I remember was waking up to a scream. I looked up to see this strange woman standing in our room wearing a robe and screaming at the top of her lungs. Then this guy runs in with a baseball bat. He yells, 'What are you doing in our apartment?' I said, 'What are you doing in my apartment?' I'm looking around for Charlotte but she wasn't there. In fact, nothing looked right. Charlotte was gone. The room was different. The pictures we had on the walls were gone. The walls themselves were different—they were wood paneling. The guy with the baseball bat asked if I was drunk. I honestly wasn't sure. Nothing made sense. He said to me, 'You wandered into the wrong apartment—now get out before we call the police.'

"I was in no position to argue. I stood up and walked backwards to the door. When I got outside, the weather had changed. There was a huge blizzard. I had no coat, no gloves or hat, just what I had on the night before.

"I looked at the apartment number on the door, it was our same apartment, only everything else was different. Someone else's name was on the mailbox. The metal railing along the corridor looked new instead of rusted, and the giant cottonwood tree outside our window was only ten feet tall.

"I kept thinking this had to be a dream. I had no idea what to do or where to go. I'm just standing there outside that apartment when I heard this voice. It said, *Go to the 7-Eleven.* The closest 7-Eleven was just down the street, about a mile from your old home."

"My *old* home?"

He nodded. "You lost the one you have now. Or you would have."

"If you hadn't saved me."

"Losing your home really affected you. Charlotte once told me that somewhere between losing your husband and your home, your spirit broke. You said, 'The next time I move I hope it's in a pine box.'"

I looked down. "I shouldn't have said that," I said, even though I hadn't yet.

"When I met Charlotte, you were living in a two-bedroom apartment near the dry cleaner. We got the apartment we did so we could be close to you."

He raked his hand back through his hair. "I walked through the storm to the 7-Eleven. I can't explain how bizarre that was. The magazines on display had pictures on their covers of people that I either didn't know or who were younger than I knew them, like Tom Hanks looking like a twelve-year-old, or President Ronald Reagan.

"As I walked in, I picked up a copy of *USA Today*. The headline was about the Romanian president and his wife being executed. The date on the paper was December 25, 1989.

"I still believed that it was all just a weird dream and that I would wake up any minute, so I got myself a cup of coffee. I was standing there drinking it when I heard an echo of Charlotte's voice that said, 'Promise me.' I looked over to the door just as you walked in. At first glance I thought you were Charlotte. You're twenty years younger than the Beth I knew, almost the same age as my wife."

It was hard for me to hear him call her that. His *wife*.

"I always thought you were pretty, it was obvious to me where Charlotte got her looks, I just didn't realize how beautiful you were. At that moment I understood why I was there.

"You were also the only thing in this time that I had to hold on to. I approached you hoping that you would recognize me, but of course you didn't. You couldn't have. You hadn't met me yet.

"I had no idea what to say to you. I mean, what am I going to do, tell you the truth? You'd have me locked up. I realized the only option I had to get in your life was to court you.

"I spent the next few days trying to figure out how to survive in 1989. I had credit cards, but there was no account behind them and I didn't want to explain why I had a card with an expiration date twenty years in the future.

"Fortunately, I had a little over a hundred dollars in my pocket, which is worth a lot more now than it is in 2008.

"I found a cheap basement apartment that didn't require a deposit, got some fake I.D. and started looking for a job.

Then one morning I was eating breakfast and reading my landlord's newspaper when I realized that I remembered most of the results of the football playoff games I was reading about. With fifty dollars left, I hitchhiked out to Wendover and started laying down bets.

"That's also where I went after Charlotte was hospitalized, it was Super Bowl Sunday, and I remembered that Joe Montana's San Francisco 49ers beat John Elway's Denver Broncos. That's how I bought the BMW."

"The big deal you were talking about was the boxing match." As bizarre as it all sounded, suddenly everything made sense.

"I didn't really follow boxing," he said, "but everyone knows about that match. It's considered one of the biggest upsets of the century." He took a deep breath. "The night you told me you were going to lose your home, I heard them talking on the radio about the upcoming Tyson-Douglas fight. I knew what I needed to do, I just needed more money than I had to wager. That's why I asked you to put me on the loan. If I had told you what I was doing, would you have agreed to it?"

"I would have thought you were crazy," I said.

"Exactly. I was just protecting you from yourself."

I shook my head. "And I thought you were a crook."

"I would have thought the same thing."

I rubbed my hand across my forehead. "I can't believe we're having this conversation. What is this voice you keep talking about?"

"It's a still, small voice I hear inside my head."

"That's how you know things?"

"Sometimes. Some things I just know. Like when I have to go back." He looked at me gravely. "*If* I'm going back."

"What do you mean *if*?"

"We have choices."

"What kinds of choices?"

"I can stay or go. It's like the train comes back to the station and I either get on it or I stay. But it's the last train. If I board it, I go back to 2008, back to Charlotte, back to whatever I have left."

I looked at him for a long time. "Will I remember you?"

He nodded. "This is now all part of your reality."

"Will you remember me?"

He frowned. "I don't know. In thirteen years, Charlotte will bring me home to meet you. That young man won't know you. He won't have crossed this time yet. He's not me yet. But maybe Christmas Eve in 2008, when we catch up . . ."

I thought it over. "And if you don't go?"

"I stay here with you and the other future disappears. All Charlotte will ever know of me is the man who loves her mother."

"So I'm competing with my own daughter for your love."

He nodded slowly. "I never meant for it to turn out like this."

"How did you think this was supposed to turn out?"

He raised his hands. "I didn't know how *any* of this would turn out. I didn't plan this when I accepted her promise. I didn't know I was going to get thrown back in time or caught in some time continuum, or whatever this is. It's not like they teach this in school, or even Sunday school for that matter. The whole thing is absurd."

"If you stay, you would remember being married to Charlotte. Just like you do now."

He nodded.

"You would see someone else take her. You'll see her fall in love with some other man who will become her husband. Could you do that?"

He looked at me sadly. "I don't know."

"Just as I'll have to see someone else take you." I looked down for a moment, then back up. I said angrily, "How could you let me fall in love with you?"

"That's not something I have control over."

"Then how could you fall in love with me?"

"How could I not?" He took my hand. "I fell in love with Charlotte because she's beautiful and caring and strong. She's like pure, sweet water. But you're the spring. How could I *not* have fallen in love with you?"

"This is wrong." I got up and walked out of the bar to the parking lot. Matthew followed me out. When I got to my car, I leaned against it. Matthew walked up behind me and put his arms around my waist. "I never meant to fall in love with you, Beth. It just happened. It doesn't mean I don't love Charlotte."

I turned around. "I can't take you from my daughter, Matthew. No matter how much losing you hurts."

"I know." He took a deep breath, exhaling slowly. "I should have just left. It would have been easier."

"Not for me. I would have blamed myself for losing you. I would have mourned you for the rest of my life."

For the next few moments we just stood there, the world passing around us, two people caught between two worlds. I touched his cheek. "How long do we have until you have to go back?"

"Christmas Eve."

"What happens on Christmas Eve?"

"I go back to the apartment. Back to 2008 to finish up what I left undone."

"Back to see Charlotte . . ." I couldn't say it. I looked down at the ground. "Three days ago I thought I was going to marry you." My eyes began to well up. I looked up into his eyes. "You knew all along."

"I'm sorry. I tried not to . . ."

I put my finger on his lips. "It's not your fault. It's what I wanted." I reached over and took his hand. "Why don't I feel guilty?"

"Because you haven't done anything wrong. Charlotte's not my wife yet."

I pressed into him, laying my head against his chest, and he wrapped his arms around me. "I know why she falls in love with you," I said.

He kissed the top of my head.

After a few minutes I said, "Christmas Eve is ten months away. What do we do with ten months?"

Neither of us spoke for a moment, then suddenly he pushed back from me. To my surprise he looked happy, as if he'd just solved some great dilemma. "What would you do if you only had ten months to live and money was no object?"

"I would spend every moment with those I love. And I would travel. I would see everything I've always wanted to see."

"That's what we'll do. We'll cheat time. We'll live more in ten months than most people do in a lifetime. We'll spend every moment together and we'll see everything."

"What about Charlotte's schooling?"

"What better education could she receive?"

"Cheat time," I said. "I like that." I looked into his face and also smiled. "The clock's ticking. What are we waiting for?"

CHAPTER

Twenty-nine

We have accumulated nothing but memories.
How happy we are.

✦ Beth Cardall's Diary ✦

Ironically, one of the things Marc said to me last summer had now become my personal mantra: I'm not going to waste a single day. It's a shame most people don't have the advantage of knowing when their time's up. If they did, they would probably live differently. They would stop trading time for trinkets. They would live like they were dying.

We had 314 days until Christmas Eve—7,536 hours. I meant to live them all.

That afternoon I sat down with Matthew and a steno pad, and we began making a list of everything we wanted to do in the time we had left. What people today call a "bucket list."

"I want to go to New York City," I said. "I've always wanted to see the Statue of Liberty and watch a real Broadway play."

"Nineteen eighty-nine," he said, searching his memories. "I think *Phantom of the Opera* has opened. You'll want to see that."

"I've never heard of it."

"You will. You'll like it. It will become the longest-running Broadway musical in history." He wrote it down on our list. "What else do you want to do?"

"I want to see Europe, or at least some of it. London, Paris, the Eiffel Tower. And Italy . . ." I paused, waiting for his scribbling to catch up. "I want to do what you did. I want to live in Italy." From his expression I could see this pleased him.

"When was the last time you were there?" I asked.

"Four years ago. We went there on our honeymoon."

It was still weird for me to hear him say things like that. It was weird imagining my six-year-old on a honeymoon.

"In June we'll fly to Monaco. The food is amazing and I need to put down a bet."

"On what?"

"It's the NBA finals. The Detroit Pistons beat the Portland Trailblazers four games to one."

I grinned. "It's so funny how you do that."

"It's like having the answers to the test in your back pocket. Fortunately, I was a young sports geek and have a head full of worthless sports trivia. But, if I was really smart, I would have learned how to make an iPod."

"What's an iPod?"

"It's an MP3 player. It plays digitized music."

"That's not helpful."

"Don't worry about it. I'll give you one someday," he said. "So we will travel the world, and when we are weary of traveling, we'll rent a villa in Anacapri, the small village at the top of Capri and we'll drink *limoncello* and go for long walks and do nothing all day but look down over the water and watch the boats come and go." He looked at me. "How does that sound?"

her for afternoon tea at the Ritz. We rode a red double-decker bus through the city and sat on top even though it rained. My favorite afternoon in London was spent wandering through the market on Portobello Road in Notting Hill. (Matthew told me that in ten years, Notting Hill would become the scene of one of Charlotte's and my favorite movies.)

At the end of the week we took a train to Stratford-upon-Avon, where we watched a presentation of *King Lear* by the Royal Shakespeare Company, ate authentic fish and chips in an English pub and stayed at a Stratford bed and breakfast.

These were the happiest of days. We had plenty of money and the only things we wanted to own were our lives. We did nothing in haste and we frequently lost track of days.

Sometime in April we headed south and crossed the channel to France. We rented a car and visited Normandy and the Omaha Beach Memorial before making our way east to Paris where we climbed both the Eiffel Tower and the bell tower at the Notre Dame Cathedral. We spent several days at the Louvre and if it hadn't been for Charlotte (how much art can a six-year-old stand?), we would have spent many more. I got to see the *Mona Lisa*, which thrilled me. I suppose it was like meeting a celebrity.

We drove through the vineyards of Bordeaux, staying in small inns and dining in family-run restaurants, and continued south to Madrid where, after we'd done all we wanted, we abandoned our car and flew to Portugal, spending two relaxing weeks in Lisbon.

"Let's pack."

"Now?"

"There is only now. We have three hundred and fourteen days. I don't want to waste a single one of them."

✦

Matthew, Charlotte and I were on a plane to New York just two days later. New York was cold and rainy and everything I hoped for. I had the best steak of my life at the famous Keens Chophouse, then, after dinner, we took a horse carriage to Broadway, where we saw the musical *Phantom of the Opera*. I thought it was the most beautiful music I had ever heard. Maybe it was just that the theme of unrequited love was so relevant to me, but I was so moved by the production that Matthew insisted we go back the next night and see it again.

We took a ferry out to the Statue of Liberty and afterward toured Ellis Island. Charlotte ate a bunless hot dog from a street vendor, had frozen hot chocolate at Serendipity 3 and spent two hours in the Barbie section of FAO Schwarz.

When we finished with New York, we flew to London. We toured Westminster Abbey and watched the changing of the guard at Buckingham Palace. We visited a handful of museums, the British Museum in Bloomsbury, the Victoria and Albert Museum and the Winston Churchill war cabinet rooms. We bought Charlotte a new dress and took

In June we flew to Monte Carlo, where we stayed at the luxurious Hôtel de Paris and lived in opulence I had only read about. Matthew put money down on the basketball playoffs, and we stayed to watch the televised tournament, though we spent most of our time at the beach.

When the tournament was over (and we had made substantially more than we had spent since we had left the States), we headed to Italy, flying directly into Florence. It wasn't until we were on Italian soil that I realized Matthew was more Italian than American. It was joyful to watch. He became more passionate and could no longer speak without using his hands. I had bought an Italian phrase book before leaving the States, and Matthew taught Charlotte and me Italian between cities.

Our first Italian destination was the small, medieval town of Arezzo, just southeast of Florence, to watch the jousting of the Saraceno. Knights in colorful armor paraded their horses into Piazza Grande preceded by flag wavers, acrobats and trumpeters. Charlotte clapped as the knights charged across the square toward their target, the Buratto, a metal armored dummy holding a shield.

We bought Charlotte colorful flags that represented each of the city's competing teams so she could wave each one in turn. Afterward, she gave them away to the Italian children seated on the bleachers around us.

The next day we took a train north to Venice, where I had my first gondola ride and taste of gelato. We went to Murano and watched them blow glass, then to Burano, where we had the most amazing seafood.

Leaving Venice, we traveled west to Verona, where Charlotte and I stood on the marble balcony of Juliet Capulet's house and waved down to Matthew, who was being our Romeo. There is a bronze statue of Juliet in the small courtyard and, as is the custom, Matthew rubbed Juliet's breast for good luck, though all he got from it was a playful slap from me.

Next we traveled to La Spezia and hiked through the five cat-infested, Kodachrome hill towns of the Cinque Terre.

In late July we went south again to Florence and spent several days visiting the sites: the Duomo and Baptistery, the Uffizi Gallery, the Accademia with Michelangelo's *David*, and the Ponte Vecchio. We stayed in a Tuscan bed and breakfast—an *agriturismo*—where the proprietor gave us bottles of his home-pressed olive oil and we sampled Tuscan cheeses to our hearts' delight.

Everywhere we went the food was extraordinary, and Matthew made sure I tried it all, from *ravioli alla crema di noci* (ravioli with cream of nut sauce) to *arancina* (little oranges). There was plenty for Charlotte to eat as well, though her favorite food was always gelato.

In Florence we rented a Vespa and the three of us drove out to the medieval town of San Gimignano, the "city of beautiful towers." Over the next week we traveled the countryside on our little scooter, stopping wherever we pleased on our way to Siena. We arrived in Siena in time to watch the Palio horse race and celebrate Charlotte's seventh birthday.

Two days later we took the Eurostar train south to Rome. We began our Roman holiday in *lo Stato della città del Vaticano* (Vatican City), where we toured St. Peter's Basilica and the Sistine Chapel, then, after lunch, took a tour through the Colosseum, the Roman Forum and Piazza Venezia. It was a full day, and I was exhausted when we finally settled down for dinner at a tourist-free, subterranean restaurant called Alle due Fontanelle. The food was spectacular though I was almost too tired to eat. I don't think my exhaustion was due just to the day; I think it was the accumulation of the last five months.

I was poking at my tiramisu when Matthew said, "Vatican City is the smallest country in the world. And Monaco is the second. I wonder what the third is."

"The Pitcairn Islands," I said.

"Where?"

"Pitcairn Islands. In the South Pacific."

He looked impressed. "How in the world did you know that?"

"It's where the *Mutiny on the Bounty* took place."

"What's the *Mutiny on the Bounty*?"

"It's an old movie. *Before* your time."

"It's always weird when you say that." He reached over and rubbed my neck. "Are you okay?"

"I think I'm ready."

"For coffee?"

I smiled. "To settle down."

"*Mamma mia, finalmente,*" he said. "You've been running me

ragged. I've been on fumes since the Cinque Terre. You're like the Energizer Bunny."

"The what?"

"Sorry, that's *after* your time."

I wagged my finger at him.

"So, why don't you and Charlotte just take it easy tomorrow, sleep in, go shopping, have fun, and I'll make arrangements for Capri. *Bene?*"

The thought of it filled me with joy. "*Bene,*" I replied. I turned to Charlotte, who was lying with her head on the table, barely keeping her eyes open. "Do you want to go live on an island?"

"Are there tigers?"

I smiled and Matthew stifled a laugh. "No, honey," I said.

"Okay."

That night as we went to bed, I said to Matthew, "There's something I don't understand. The younger you . . ." I wasn't sure how to ask this. "In nineteen ninety you were ten years old."

"Right."

"That means you're still in Italy. But you're also here now. Are there two of you?"

"I really don't know. I'm not sure how this works. But I'm pretty sure that my parents are in Sorrento."

"What if you accidentally run into them?"

"Then there will be a clash of time continuums and the world and universe will come to an abrupt end."

I stared at him. "Really?"

He burst out laughing. "No. I just saw that on a science

fiction show once. They wouldn't know me, of course, any more than if a thirty-year-old Charlotte walked up to you right now and asked for directions."

"But what if you see yourself?"

A slight smile crossed his face. "That would be cool."

CHAPTER

Thirty

*The world would be a better place if people
and countries learned this one lesson:
Desiring something doesn't make it yours.*

✦ Beth Cardall's Diary ✦

There is something you may be wondering. Through those ten months together, dozens of cities and thousands of miles, Matthew and I were never intimate. I know, in today's world, that might not seem plausible, but our situation was not out of today's world. I'm not saying that there weren't times that abstinence wasn't agonizing. That would be a lie. And we were certainly affectionate. But as much as I loved and wanted Matthew, he was still my daughter's future husband. And that made all the difference. Love gives you strength to do what's right. Even when it's hard.

Matthew and I never talked about our desires, or even our chasteness, for that matter. It was just understood. Though once, in a lighter moment, I said to him, "You know, if I had your baby and it was a boy and then you went back to 2008, your son would be your brother-in-law."

He thought about it for a moment then said, "That's just bizarre."

"Absolutely bizarre," I said.

We both started laughing.

CHAPTER

Thirty-one

By grace or oversight,
there are corners of Eden that God left on this earth.

✦ Beth Cardall's Diary ✦

Capri is a dream, a jagged chunk of limestone that juts out of the cobalt blue Tyrrhenian Sea just west of the Sorrentine peninsula. Julius Caesar so coveted the beautiful island that he traded fertile farmland for the rock. Since that time it has been a favorite of artists from around the world, from the great Russian writer Gorky to the French classical composer Claude Debussy, who even named one of his preludes "Les collines d'Anacapri" in homage to Anacapri— a small commune nestled atop the Capri mountains. It was the perfect setting for our life at that time, a dreamscape. A symphony.

Matthew had found a villa for us in Anacapri. The wide, spacious home was already furnished and had white stucco walls hung with paintings from local artists and vibrant ceramics. Behind the home there was a large, terra-cotta–tiled terrace that overlooked the sea. The outside walls were also whitewashed, though mostly covered with purple bougainvillea, a flowering plant that climbed the walls like ivy. The yard beyond our villa was lush with cyprus, yellow oleanders and lemon trees that produced fruit as large as grapefruits.

As I look back over my life, I have never been so happy as I was in Capri, and the days passed all too quickly. Unfortunately, happiness came with an expiration date.

✦ Beth Cardall's Diary ✦

October came. There was a particular evening I will never forget. We had spent the day in a small motorboat exploring inlets around the island until we were all exhausted and sunburned. We stopped near the port for dinner, then came home, where Matthew put Charlotte to bed and I retired to the terrace, looking out over the shimmering sea. The air was cool and moist and filled with the sweet scent of the Capri oleanders.

I just sat content to do nothing, my thoughts as vague and drifting as the sea. My reverie was broken by Matthew's voice.

"May I join you?" He carried a porcelain teacup in each hand.

I looked up and smiled. "Of course."

He set the tea on the small, tile-topped table next to me and sat down, sharing with me the view. "It's beautiful tonight," he said.

"It's always beautiful," I said.

"*Sempre bella,*" he repeated softly. "You've been quiet today. What are you thinking?"

"It's the anniversary of Marc's death."

"I didn't know. I'm sorry."

"I'm not," I said sadly. I looked at him. "I wonder what

would have happened if he hadn't come down with cancer. Would he have ever told me? Or would my whole marriage have just been a lie?" I took a sip of tea and let the moment fall into silence. "My life would have been different," I said softly, downplaying the enormity of the understatement. It was a few more minutes before I asked, "How do you and Charlotte meet?"

He turned back toward the sea. "We meet at a friend's party. She was with some of her friends. I was a goner the moment I saw her. You should have seen her." He smiled. "I guess you will."

"Are you happily married?"

He hesitated. "We are very happy. Charlotte taught me how to love. As I told you on our first date, she's my everything. But watching her suffer through the cancer . . ." He stopped. "It was like having my heart peeled one layer at a time." He set down his tea and turned toward me. "I fear the future, Beth. I need to go back to it, but I fear it more than I could ever tell you."

"When do we go back?" I asked.

He took a long drink of his tea following the golden horizon with his gaze. "We'll know when it's time," he said. "You'll know."

CHAPTER

Thirty-two

*The story is told of a gentleman who was reading his
newspaper aboard a train when the conductor shouted,
"The brakes are out, we're picking up speed and we're going
to crash into the station—everyone off the train!"
The passengers began jumping off. As the conductor himself
was about to leap he looked at the gentleman who was still
casually reading his paper. "Aren't you going to jump?"
he asked. The gentleman replied, "I'm going to wait
until I reach the station to decide."
I should have jumped before the train got moving too fast.*

✦ Beth Cardall's Diary ✦

The next two months passed like a dream—but all dreams come with the expectation of waking. As *the day* (as I began to call it) came closer, I found myself struggling more and more with my decision to let Matthew go, and a battle waged in my heart. *Didn't I deserve happiness too? Didn't I deserve love? Haven't I given everything for my daughter? Doesn't she want me to be happy too?*

One afternoon I was watching Matthew teach Charlotte Italian when I found myself resenting the time he spent with her. I found myself resenting *her*.

Jealousy is as subtle as a weed. I didn't notice its first inroads into my heart, but it was there, filling in the cracks of our relationship, growing stronger each day and cleaving us apart. I wasn't just resenting her, I was resenting *them*, the future couple. More and more I found myself angry at Matthew. *Why wasn't he fighting for me? Why didn't he at least ask me to stay? Had he ever really loved me?*

It was mid-December. Matthew had gone down to Capri to bring back fresh fish for supper and had taken Charlotte with him. They were gone several hours longer than I had expected, and as twilight fell, I grew angrier with each tick of the clock. When they finally arrived home, I blew up at him. "Where have you been?"

"Amore," he said. *"Mi dispiace,* the fisherman was a friend of mine and he offered to take Charlotte through the Blue Grotto."

"While I just sit here alone wondering where you are?"

He leaned over and whispered to Charlotte and she ran off to her bedroom. Then he just looked at me, carefully reading me. "I'm sorry. I didn't think you would care."

"You didn't think I would care or you just didn't care." I stormed out of the room to my bedroom, slammed the door and threw myself on the bed.

A minute later he knocked on the door even though it had no lock. "Beth, can we talk?"

"Vai!" I shouted.

He didn't speak for a moment, then he said gently, "May I please come in?"

I was crying hard. He opened the door, then walked to the side of the bed and knelt down next to me.

I said, "Why don't you want to be with me? Why are you spending so much time with her?"

He was quiet for a moment, then replied. "Beth, I'm not just saying goodbye to you." He took my hand. "When I go back, there is no time left with her. This is the last time I will have with my wife."

I had been so selfishly caught up in my loss and in my time that I had not even considered what he was going back to. I was filled with enormous shame. "I'm sorry. I'm so sorry. Please forgive me."

"You don't need to be forgiven," he said. "I would never hold your love for me against you."

He lay down on the bed next to me and put his arm across my back. When I could speak, I said, "It's time."

"Are you sure?"

"Yes." I didn't want to look at him. "I'm so afraid."

He put both of his arms around me. He held me while I cried. When I had finally calmed, he said, "We'll leave Monday." He kissed me on the cheek, then got up and left the room.

As soon as the door shut, I began again to cry. I could already feel him slipping away. He wasn't mine and I was terrified to lose him.

CHAPTER

Thirty-three

*I have wondered if those who say
"it is better to have loved and lost than never to have
loved at all," have ever lost their loved.*

✦ Beth Cardall's Diary ✦

An hour later Matthew returned. He lay down next to me and put his arms around me and held me through the night. Usually, when my heart is wracked with pain, I seek sleep to escape, but not this time. Pain or bliss, I didn't want to miss any of his touch. I just lay in his arms feeling his body against mine, absorbing his warmth as if I could somehow store it. I don't know when I fell asleep, but when I woke the next morning, the sun had already climbed above the Sorrentine mountains. Matthew rolled over and kissed me. "I'd like to take you out to dinner tonight. Just the two of us."

"I'd like that."

"I'll be in Capri most of the day making arrangements. I'll ask Nonna Sonia to tend Charlotte tonight. Okay?"

"Grandma" Sonia was our cleaning lady, though she seemed more like family than housemaid.

"Okay," I said.

I spent most of the day with Charlotte. I needed to tell her that we were leaving. In the early afternoon we took the chairlift to the top of Mt. Solaro. From the mountain vista we could see 360° around the island clear to Naples and south to the Amalfi coast. I bought her an orange Fanta and we sat down on a bench.

"We're very high up," I told Charlotte. "This is the highest place on Capri."

"Is it the highest place in the world?"

I shook my head. "No. Only our world." I pulled her in close to me. "It's time to go home, sweetheart." I realized that she might not be sure where that was anymore. "Home to Utah."

She looked down but said nothing.

"Did you like living here?"

"I want to always live here," she said. "With Matthew."

I looked down at her. "Don't ever forget that. Your wish may come true."

That night I wore a hand-sewn white linen dress that Matthew had bought for me from a tailor in Anacapri. We went to a small restaurant about twenty minutes from the piazza, away from the tourists and their haunts.

It was hard finding words adequate for the moment, so we ate. I asked Matthew to order for me and we had ravioli in sage butter and tender steak cutlets with parmesan and rucola. We had finished our meals and were drinking prosecco from beautiful crystal glasses when Matthew said, "I have something for you." He reached under the table and brought out a small, cedarwood box.

I looked at the box then up into his eyes. "I want you to open it for me."

He held the box in front of me and pulled back its lid. Inside the velvet-lined box was a ghostly blue cameo pendant attached to a gold rope.

I put my hand over my mouth.

"I bought it in Positano. I was just waiting for the right moment."

I just stared at it. It was beautiful. The cameo had the profile of a woman carved in an abalone shell, set in a gold bezel.

"Do you like it?"

"Oh, Matthew."

He lifted the necklace from the box. "Let's see how it looks on you." He reached around my neck and connected the clasp. I suppose that the simplest of things, when facing extinction, become of utmost worth. The touch of his hands on my neck filled me with exquisite pleasure. He sat back and I looked down at the cameo, touching it against my breast. "Thank you."

"It's something for you to remember me by."

He said this as if it were possible that I could forget him. "I don't need anything to remember you by or this time we've had together. I could never forget." I looked into his eyes. "Do you know what I fear most?"

He shook his head. "No, *amore*."

"That you won't remember me."

The next morning we packed our necessities. A little after noon, a truck arrived outside the villa, and Matthew's two friends, Nonna Sonia's grandsons, Salvatore and Dario, helped us with our baggage and drove us down the mountain to the port of Capri. Several large boats had docked in the marina that hour and the city was crowded with tourists.

Using handcarts, our friends lugged our baggage through the crowd along the long, wooden pier to a ferry on the far end of the Capri dock.

We kissed them both goodbye, then climbed aboard the boat minutes before it pulled away from the dock. I never looked back at my beloved Capri. I couldn't.

In Sorrento, Matthew got us a cab and we went to the train station, where we boarded the train to Rome.

It was late, nearly eleven o'clock, when we disembarked at the Rome Termini and checked into the Ambasciatori Palace Hotel on the Via Veneto near the U.S. Embassy and the Church of the Cappuccini with its four thousand sleeping residents.

We slept for much of the next morning, Matthew transacted more business downstairs, and it was afternoon when we went out as a family into the city for our last night in Italy.

At twilight we ate dinner in the Piazza Navona with its three Bernini statues. It was a sullen time and only Charlotte had much to say, as she ran excitedly between the fountains, artists, merchants and mimes on the cobblestone surface.

Matthew and I finished our cappuccinos, then, taking Charlotte's hand, walked the crowded sidewalks about a half-mile to the Trevi Fountain, the final outlet of the ancient Roman aqueducts.

You can hear the Trevi waters before you reach the fountain, which is always crowded after dusk. At night the blue, illuminated waters shimmer seductively beneath the statuary, casting golden webs across its marble facade. The central figure of the Trevi is a trident-wielding Neptune, the Greek god of water, flanked by two Tritons, one trying to rein in a wild seahorse, the other leading a docile one, symbolic of the contrasting moods of the sea.

Holding tightly to Charlotte's hands, we walked down the crowded stairway to the marble retaining wall of the pool. The churning waters dulled the sounds of the crowds and I looked over at Matthew, who was staring at the fountain, lost in thought. Then I saw him reach into his pocket and bring out coins. He leaned close to me to speak.

"The legend says that if you throw one coin into the fountain, you will return to Rome. If you throw two, you will find love." He held out the coins.

I shook my head. "Then I don't want them." My eyes welled up with tears as I turned away from him.

"Beth." He grabbed my shoulders and pulled me around to look into my eyes.

"I've found love, Matthew. I don't want to love someone else and I don't ever want to come back here without you."

For a moment he just looked at me, his beautiful eyes mirroring my sadness. Then he said, "If this is what I've brought to your life—then I've failed. I promised to come back to take care of you, not to take you. I came to bring you hope."

I turned away from him. I looked down for a long while, then up at the pulsing theater around me, the vibrant, bois-terous crowds—the camera-toting tourists, the fresh-faced students in their Levi's and sneakers, the young American women with hopeful eyes, the Italian women with their scolding lips, the Gypsy boys selling roses—each of them playing their roles, each playing out their parts. And then I grasped what it had to teach me, that life would go on. Just as the fountain's water flowed each night for different eyes, with or without him, my life would still flow and churn and bubble. I looked out over the waters, then back into Mat-thew's eyes and put out my hand. "I want two coins."

He grasped my hand as he gave them to me. I turned my back to the fountain and threw both coins over my shoulder.

"*Brava*," he said, his eyes moist.

"Let's go home," I said.

✦

We got up early the next morning and took a cab to Leonardo da Vinci airport. Our flight was direct to New York's JFK, with a connection to Salt Lake City. We passed through customs, then rechecked our luggage and boarded a new flight. We arrived in Utah at around six o'clock on the same day we left. I habitually did the calculations—it was two in the morning in Italy.

It wasn't snowing when we landed, but it was freezing cold and the landscape was white beneath a blanket of snow.

Roxanne and Ray picked us up outside the terminal. Oddly, even Roxanne, for once, seemed subdued, as if she sensed that there was something to be mourned. As we drove up the quiet, holiday-dressed street to my home, our ten months already seemed like a dream. I couldn't believe our time together was gone. You can cheat time, but it will find you.

CHAPTER

Thirty-four

Three days left.

✦ Beth Cardall's Diary ✦

We moved slowly those last days, as if the speed of our actions could somehow slow time. To my disappointment, Matthew was gone for most of the afternoon of the twenty-second and the morning of the twenty-third. On the afternoon of the twenty-third, he brought me into the bedroom to talk. There were practical matters to be discussed, he said, which felt grim to me, like the planning of one's own funeral. As I look back on it all, it was the most interesting conversation of my life.

We sat on the floor facing each other. Matthew had a large, accordion-style file folder brimming with what I would discover were certificates and documents. Matthew spoke with the stoic demeanor of a financial advisor.

"What I'm giving you now is all the financial information you will ever need. This morning I paid off this home, so you own it free and clear. You still have more than two million dollars left in your accounts. Over the last two days I have divided them into funds that will do well over the next eighteen years. There are a few companies you need to invest in that haven't started or gone public yet. One of them is called Google. They'll go public in 1996. The other is YouTube in 2005. YouTube will be a private fund, so I've given you special instructions on whom to contact. It's very important that you invest the exact amounts at the times I have written down.

"If you do what I say, you will be wealthy beyond your wildest imagination. Do not, I repeat, do not let anyone change or touch these accounts. There will be people who will try to talk you out of it, or think they know better. They don't. The best they have is an educated guess. I'm not guessing, I've read the last page. I know how the story ends. Promise me you will do exactly what I say."

"I promise."

"Remember how I tricked you into signing me on as a cosignatory on your home-equity loan?"

I nodded.

"Don't ever do that again. There will be temptations. There will be fools. Money attracts fools. Do not give in to them."

He pulled out an envelope. "This is a fund for Charlotte's education. She's going to major in art history and will decide to attend the University of Utah mostly to be near you, so this fund will ensure that you will have more than enough for school, books and lodging."

He replaced the envelope and pulled out another. "This packet right here is time-sensitive. Do not touch these funds until the dates I've written down, then be sure to take all the money out. The dates I've written are generalities, the best I can remember, so if they're off a bit, don't worry about it. They're close enough."

"If you want to buy something big, like a mansion or yacht or something . . ."

I stopped him. "Why would I want those things?"

"I'm not saying you will, just that any big expenditure needs to come out of this fund. This is your liquid fund. Don't ever spend more than this account or you'll kill the golden goose. People get rich and they go nuts and lose it all. Most lottery winners end up bankrupt. It's the norm. As long as you don't leave the path I set for you, you'll be safe. Step off it, even once, and you may be back pressing suit coats and clipping coupons." He looked me in the eyes. "Do you understand?"

"I understand."

"Good." He sighed and pulled out another small packet. "This might seem a little selfish, but this fund is for Charlotte and me. It will be worth several million when it matures. We can't access it until we are thirty. I did that on purpose, I didn't want to mess up the future I'm stepping back into and I didn't want to ruin Charlotte. It's best if Charlotte doesn't know about it until it matures."

"Okay."

"Now this checkbook, the green one, is what I call your Mad Money account. It's an interest-bearing checking account. This is what you are going to gamble with. I made a list of all the Super Bowl and NBA championship winners for the next fifteen years. Just keep gambling the money and turn it over. Never gamble more than half of it at once, just in case I made a mistake." He took my hand. "Does all this make sense?"

I nodded.

"I know it's a lot, but I wrote everything down. This is your new job, managing your money. Promise me you will do only what I've told you to do."

"I promise."

"As long as you stay in the pen, the wolves won't get you. Step outside . . ."

"I'm dinner."

"Exactly." He breathed out and pushed the file aside. "Okay, enough about money. There are other things you should know about the future. I made this for you." He lifted a small steno notepad he'd had at his side. "I've written down some things I think you'll find helpful. Some are important, some are just interesting. For instance, you know the group Milli Vanilli?"

"The singers," I said. "They just won a Grammy for best new artist."

"Yeah, well they're fake. It's not really them singing."

"What?"

"It will come out later this year." He turned a few pages. "Here's something six or seven years away. Harry Potter is going to be really big, so if you want, secure the dot-com address as soon as you can. You can sell it back to them. The author's going to be a billionaire, so don't settle for less than a hundred thousand dollars. Trust me."

"Who's Harry Potter?"

"He's a fictional character in a series of books about a boy wizard."

"A wizard?"

He nodded. "It's going to be big." He leafed through a few more pages. "Oh, this is very, very important. Stay out of New York City, actually, don't fly at all, on September 11th, 2001."

"Why?"

"That's one I can't tell you. Just trust me." He turned a few more pages. "We'll go to war twice with Iraq. The second time we'll be looking for weapons of mass destruction, but they'll never find any. But they will eventually find Saddam Hussein."

"Who's that?"

"You'll find out. I filled this whole book with information like that. The bottom line is, over the next two decades you're going to hear doomsday scenarios, dire predictions, 'blood will run in the streets' propaganda. None of it will happen. Be at peace, the world will go on."

He handed me the book and the file folder. "Protect this information, don't tell anyone about it, not Roxanne, not even Charlotte. You don't want that responsibility and you don't want to screw up the future." He reached into his pocket and took out a small brass key and handed it to me. "Just in case there's a fire or something and these copies are destroyed, there are backup copies of everything in this safe deposit box. It's at the bank where we took out your home-equity loan."

"Thank you," I said.

"That's why I'm here, isn't it?" He stood. "Oh, one more

thing. When I come over for Charlotte's twenty-first birth-day party, don't point out that my fly is open in front of everyone. It was really embarrassing."

"I really did that?"

"Yeah, you did."

"Sorry."

CHAPTER

Thirty-five

Make no mistake—the day of reckoning always arrives on time. We can deny the approaching reef, but we can't deny the collision.

✦ Beth Cardall's Diary ✦

The morning of December 24, I was a mess. I woke crying and rolled over into Matthew's arms. He held me but didn't speak. I knew his heart was breaking as well. I tried to keep busy that morning by doing normal things, as if there was anything normal at all about the day. I made waffles for breakfast, forgetting that Charlotte couldn't eat them, and neither Matthew nor I were hungry.

Around noon I dropped Charlotte off at Roxanne's under the guise of Santa preparations then came back home. Matthew was sitting in the living room. He was tying his shoes.

"Do you need to pack?" I asked.

"For what?"

"Sorry," I said. "This is new to me."

"Do you want to get some lunch?"

"I'm not really hungry," I said, "but I'll keep you company."

"I'm not hungry either, I just need to get out of here before I lose my mind."

"Okay," I said, "let's go."

The streets were insanely crowded with last-minute Christmas shoppers. We went to a small French café in Holladay, but the wait was more than an hour, so we took our drinks and salads to go and drove to a nearby park. We sat at a metal picnic table beneath an open canopy, our breath freezing before us.

We talked mostly about the last ten months; our favorite cities and restaurants, the size of lemons in Capri, the glass factory in Murano and seafood in Burano, and laughed hysterically at Niccola, the cute little Italian man who led us through Pompeii, called the other guides "idjits" and finished each declaration with "thank you." We talked about everything except the clock that was ticking down. We didn't need to. I swear I could hear it.

"Are you set on the story?" he asked me.

I nodded. "Your grandmother died last night in Sorrento, so you left suddenly to get back in time for the funeral. While you are there, you are killed in a car accident."

Matthew nodded. "The fewer details you give the better. Do you think you'll convince Roxanne? You may have to pretend to cry."

"I haven't stopped crying since we left Capri and you haven't even left yet. I don't think it will be a problem."

He frowned. "How do you think Charlotte will take it?"

"Not well. But she'll survive. It's not the first time she's lost someone close to her. I'll take care of her." I rolled my cup in my hands. "Is there anything I should know about Charlotte?"

"Nothing that I haven't already told you."

"How about boys . . ."

"You shouldn't get too involved. You might scare her away from me. Just be yourself."

I nodded.

We got home around three. I was so emotionally drained that I decided to take a short nap. I woke to Matthew gently shaking me. "It's time," he said softly. I sat up. "What? What time is it?"

"It's six."

My eyes immediately filled with tears. "Why didn't you wake me?"

He kissed my cheek. "It's better this way." He knelt on the bed next to me and put his arms around me and we held each other. After a few minutes he pulled away from me, still holding my hand. "Let's do it."

We walked out to my car and drove just a few miles down the road, a few blocks past the 7-Eleven where we'd first met. At his direction I pulled off from the boulevard down a side street. "It's just up ahead," he said, "where that red car's parked."

I drove forward and pulled up to the curb behind the car. "Here?"

"It's this apartment building," he said, tilting his head toward a two-story, flat-roofed structure.

"Which number is it? I can save you some time when you and Charlotte go apartment hunting." *Stupid thing to say.*

"Two-zero-seven, the one on the side by the stairwell."

I looked at the door. I don't know what I was expecting it to look like, but there was nothing special about it.

"It looks like any other door," I said.

He shrugged. "I look like any other guy."

"Not to me."

He reached over and took my hand. "Are you afraid?"

"Yes."

"So am I."

"Why aren't I there when my daughter dies?"

He looked down. "I guess Charlotte didn't want you to see her go."

"Why?"

"Because you've hurt too much over her already." He leaned over and put his arms around me and held me. After a few minutes he leaned back and looked into my eyes. "I will always love you."

"You can't promise me that. Not like this." I buried my head on his shoulder. He just held me again.

"Beth, are you sure this is what you want?"

"Please, don't tempt me. I want my girl to be happy. I want you to be happy with her."

"You're always looking after her."

"That's why you're here, isn't it?" I rubbed my hand over his back. "The next time you see me, I'll be fourteen years older. I won't be so pretty."

"I've seen you in nineteen years. You're still beautiful."

Neither of us spoke after that. I just clung to him. A few minutes later he sighed. "It's time," he said. "I can't put this off any longer."

I slowly released him. "Take care of my girl."

"I promise."

He opened the car door and stepped out, then leaned back through the window. *"Ciao, bella."*

I wiped my eyes. *"Ciao."* He turned and began to walk away when I shouted, "Matthew!"

He stopped. I got out of the car and ran to him and we embraced. "Please don't forget me. Promise me."

"I don't know if I can."

"I can't live with that. I can sacrifice you for her, I can sacrifice my love, but I can't live with you never knowing that we had this time." I looked up at him pleadingly. "You once said, 'You can't believe what I can promise.' You promised her. Promise me. Please, just say it."

He looked into my eyes then ran his finger over my cheek. "I promise."

"Okay," I said, "Okay." I stepped away from him, still holding his hand. *"Ci vediamo."* I stepped back until we dropped each other's hands.

"Bye."

He turned and I watched him walk up toward the apartment. He looked back once more and gave me a short wave. I wiped my eyes and waved back. Then I went back to the car and went to get my Charlotte.

CHAPTER

Thirty-six

They say that you can never go back home again.
But it's not the home that changes, it's the traveler.

✴ Beth Cardall's Diary ✴

Matthew tentatively grasped the doorknob, unsure of what lay behind it and even more unsure of how he would respond. He thought back to the previous Christmas Eve, when the strange couple had forced him out of the apartment with a baseball bat. The idea of encountering them again was far less frightening than the prospect of finding Charlotte in bed, struggling to live—to witness her death. Or, had she already passed? He looked back to the road, to maybe catch a glimpse of Beth's car, but it was gone.

He turned the knob. He was not surprised to find the door unlocked, for the same reason he knew he was to be there. He slowly opened the door, took a deep breath and stepped inside, crossing a threshold of time and sealing the past behind him.

He glanced around the quiet room. The apartment was exactly the way he remembered it. Their furniture was back. The wood paneling was gone and the walls were painted vanilla yellow, adorned with their pictures. On the front room wall, above the sofa, was Charlotte's bridal picture. He was back. Two thousand eight was back. He looked to the open bedroom door and cautiously took a step toward it. Then he heard a voice. "Matthew?"

Just then Charlotte stepped out of the bedroom, her head cocked to one side as she fastened an earring. She wore a bright Christmas sweater tight enough to accent the small bump of her waist. "Where have you been, love?"

He just stared at her and her stomach. "You're okay."

She smiled. "Of course I am, silly. I told you it was just a little late afternoon morning sickness. Where have you been?"

He stared at her. "I, uh, went for a walk."

"Without a coat?"

He walked up and threw his arms around her. "Charlotte."

She laughed. "Careful, you'll muss me up. Now hurry and change, we'll be late for Mom's party."

"Of course." He went into the bedroom to dress. Some things in the room were the same, some different. There were new clothes in the closet mixed in with clothes he recognized. He put on some corduroy jeans and a sweater he'd never seen before. Charlotte was waiting by the door holding a small wrapped package when he walked out.

She looked him over. "I love that sweater. Didn't Mom give that to you for your birthday?"

"I don't remember."

"I think she did. She'll be glad you're wearing it. Do you have the keys?"

"No. Where are they?"

"Where we always put them."

Matthew went into the kitchen and was relieved to find that the keys were in the same drawer they always were. He looked around the room. It had changed. It was decorated in Tuscan design.

"Come on, Matthew, we're late."

"I'm coming," he said.

Charlotte took his hand as they walked out of the apartment. "That was so sweet of you, hugging me like that. I don't know what's gotten into you, but don't let it out."

"I was just thinking how I'd never get over it if something happened to you."

"What made you think of that?"

"I don't know," he said. He looked back at her. She looked different now. He could still see the little girl in her. "How old were you when you were diagnosed with celiac?"

"That's random," she said. "I don't know. Just little, I think six."

He nodded. "Six," he said. "Of course."

Snow was lightly falling as they walked out to their car. Matthew opened the door for her, then climbed in the driver's side, turned on the heater and pulled out of the apartment's parking lot. The streets were mostly deserted and he pulled into the turn lane at the first intersection they came to. Charlotte looked over at him. "Where are you going?"

"I thought we were going to your Mom's."

"This isn't the way to Mom's."

He turned through the intersection, then pulled over to

the side of the road. "You know, I have a really bad headache. Would you mind driving?"

"I'm sorry. Of course."

Matthew climbed out of the car and walked around while Charlotte slid over to the driver's seat. He climbed in and fastened his seat belt.

"I didn't know you weren't feeling well," Charlotte said. "Are you feeling up to this party?"

"I'll be fine."

Charlotte pulled out into the street, made a U-turn, then drove south up toward Big Cottonwood Canyon. Ten minutes later they pulled into a gated subdivision of large, exclusive homes. The road was blocked by a wide red-and-yellow-striped gate arm festively strung with Christmas lights, next to a security guard's shack. The uniformed guard opened his window. "Merry Christmas."

"Merry Christmas to you," Charlotte said. "We're visiting my mother, the Breinholts."

Breinholts?

"Just a minute, please." The guard lifted a phone, spoke to someone, then waved them forward as the gate arm rose. A minute later Charlotte pulled into the circular driveway of a large stucco and rock home near the end of the subdivision.

The home was a towering, gabled structure with a massive rock chimney and large gaslight fixtures across the front of the house that flickered against the gray winter sky. Even in winter the landscaping was lush, and large pines in the yard had been professionally wrapped in twinkling Christmas lights. Matthew looked at it in awe. "How many years has she lived here?"

"Ever since she married Kevin."

He looked at her. *Kevin?*

"How long ago was that," Charlotte said to herself, "fourteen years ago? I think I was ten or eleven."

Matthew looked over the structure. "That is one big house," he said to himself.

Charlotte stopped the car beneath the stone portico leading to the home's entrance. "You sure you're feeling okay? How far did you go on your walk?"

You have no idea, he thought. "A ways."

"Well, if you need to leave, just let me know. Mom will understand. By the way, Kevin had some cancers removed from his arm, so he has a bunch of bandages, in case you're wondering."

"Is he okay?"

"They were just being cautious. You know how Mom is when it comes to cancer."

They got out of the car and walked up beneath a long portico to the front door—a tall, arched, carved-wood door with heavy brass metal fixtures. Charlotte pushed it open into the bright, marble-floored foyer, and they were met by a rush of light and warmth. "Mom, Dad, we're here," she called.

A well-dressed, elegant-looking man, with gray temples walked into the foyer. He wore a broad, pleasant smile. "Charlotte, Matthew, Merry Christmas!"

"Merry Christmas, Daddy," Charlotte said, running to him. They hugged.

"How are you, Matt?"

"Great," he said. "Merry Christmas." He motioned to the bandages on Kevin's arm. "You okay?"

"It's nothing. All benign, but thanks for asking. You need to try some of my wassail. I think I finally nailed it."

"I'd love to."

Kevin said to Charlotte, "Your mom is still putting her face on. She's been up there for nearly an hour. Maybe with you here she'll finally come down."

"I don't know why she does that," Charlotte said. "It's just us."

"I told her that. But you know your beautiful mom, she always wants to look her best. I'll let her know you're here." He walked to the foot of the circular staircase and shouted, "Beth, the kids are here."

CHAPTER

Thirty-seven

*Just as a journey of a thousand miles ends with a few steps,
a wait of decades ends with a few seconds.
The time has come.*

✦ Beth Cardall's Diary ✦

I was sitting on the bed when Kevin called upstairs.

"I'll be right down," I shouted. I walked back into the bathroom and took another look in the mirror. Even if I could hide the puffiness of my eyes, I couldn't hide the wrinkles. If he did remember, would I look old to him? Of course I would. To him I was nearly twenty years older. He would look the same as he did last week when he came over to help Kevin install the new television downstairs.

I can't hide up here forever, I told myself. I took a deep breath, then walked out of the room, down the hall to the stairs. Charlotte and Matthew were in the foyer below. They both looked up at me. "Merry Christmas, Mom," Charlotte said.

"Merry Christmas, sweetie. You look darling. How are you feeling?"

"I'm fine."

I turned to Matthew and said a little too formally, "Merry Christmas, Matthew."

"Merry Christmas, Mom."

When I got to the bottom of the stairs, I kissed Charlotte, then Matthew. "You need to try Kevin's wassail," I said to them.

"He offered," Matthew said. "I was just making my way to the kitchen."

"Always something new," Charlotte said. "Fortunately, everything he makes is fabulous."

The door chime rang, and before I could even take a step toward the door, it swung open and Roxanne stepped inside. "Anybody home?"

"Rox," I said.

"Baby doll." She ran over to hug me. "Merry Christmas, oh, don't you look delicious. Ray, you just keep your eyes to yourself."

Ray was a dozen feet behind her, huffing a little and leaning against his cane. "Merry Christmas, Beth."

"Merry Christmas, Ray. Kevin's in the kitchen. There's cold beer in the refrigerator."

"I'm on it."

"What is that you're wearing?" Roxanne said, looking at my cameo. "Is that new?"

"No. It's very old. I got it back in Capri."

"Is it—" she stopped herself. Roxanne rarely practiced restraint, but the topic of Capri had always been off limits.

I looked over and noticed that Matthew was staring at me. "It is beautiful," he said. "When did you get it?"

"Many years ago. A dear friend gave it to me."

Roxanne said to Matthew, "Hello, you handsome Italian devil. Give me a kiss."

Matthew grinned. "Hi, Rox." He kissed her cheek.

"Always the cheek," she said. "Always the cheek. Just once

I'd like a big smack on the lips. And look at you girl," she said, patting Charlotte's stomach. "You look just precious with a bun in the oven. And what is that heavenly smell? What is Kevin up to this year?"

"No matter what Daddy makes, you know it's going to be good," Charlotte said.

"He's trying something new this year," I said. "Italian."

"*Mamma mia*," Rox said, "I just love Italian. Everything Italian. You too," she said to Matthew. "I should have married me one of them."

"Should have," Ray said from the kitchen.

"Let me take your coat."

I hung her coat in the hall closet, then glanced over at Matthew, who was now walking around the house looking at pictures with one hand in his pocket, a glass of wassail in the other. Kevin called from the kitchen, "Beth, would you mind serving the antipasti?"

"Of course." I went to the kitchen. Kevin had filled a plate with his bacon-wrapped scallops impaled with toothpicks. I lifted one and popped it into my mouth. "Delicious, honey."

Kevin smiled at me. "Thanks."

I lifted the tray. "Scallops, anyone?"

"I'll have one of those," said Ray. "Or ten."

"Matthew?"

"Sure. Thanks." He took two. "One for Charlotte," he said.

"She can't have one," I said.

"She can't?"

"You know . . . pregnant women and shellfish."

"Oh. Sorry. I forgot." He started to put it back.

"No, keep it. A strapping young man like you can have them both." I started to walk away, then stopped. "Matthew, would you mind grabbing the napkins?"

"Sure." He looked around. "Where are they?"

"Where you put them away last time," I said. He didn't move. I pointed toward a drawer. "Next to the dishwasher."

"Right," he said. He opened the drawer and brought out a handful.

Twenty minutes later Kevin shouted, "Dinner's ready. Everyone to the dining room."

Charlotte and I helped Kevin carry the last of the platters to the dining room, where we all congregated.

"Where do you want us to sit, Mom?" Charlotte asked.

"Kevin, you're at the head. Rox and Ray, you sit right there by me, Matthew, you and Charlotte sit right here."

When we were seated, Kevin took my hand. "Would you mind saying grace, dear?"

"I'd love to, thank you." I bowed my head. "Dear Lord, thank you for this beautiful Christmas season and for Christmases past. Thank you for our many blessings and abundance. Thank you for family. We ask thee to bless this food to our good and us to thy service. Amen."

There was a chorus of amens, the loudest, of course, being Roxanne's. Kevin said, "*Buon appetito.*" He turned to Matthew. "Did I say that right?"

"Like a native," Matthew said.

"What have you made us?" Charlotte asked.

"I thought I would try Italian this year. *Prima piatto,*" he said, slaughtering the language, "Manicotti. And for our favorite girl's special diet, manicotti wrapped in spinach, sausage soup and veal Parmesan."

Charlotte smiled. "Thanks, Daddy."

"My pleasure, honey."

Kevin ladled sausage soup into our bowls. When everyone had been served, Charlotte asked Roxanne, "How's Jan?"

"You know, busy 'momming' Ethan junior. He's five now."

"We're Facebook friends," Charlotte said. "She posts pictures of Ethan almost every day."

"The boy's a monster," Roxanne said. "And he's only in kindergarten."

"He's not a monster," Ray said, putting a spoon into his mouth.

"He's a monster," Rox said, pointing a fork at Ray. "You give birth to a ten-pounder, then you can talk." She turned back to Charlotte. "When I married Mr. Right, I didn't know his first name was *Always*."

Ray shook his head.

Charlotte laughed. "I always knew she'd make the best mother. She was such a fun babysitter. I was sorry to hear that she wasn't coming back for the holidays. Christmas isn't the same without her."

"She never visits anymore at Christmas. Go figure, especially now that her last name is Klaus. I never thought my daughter would be Mrs. Klaus. I was heartbroken when I found out she wasn't coming, wasn't I, Ray?"

"Heartbroken," he said.

"I guess that Tim is just so busy with work right now. He's now a partner in the clinic, so he has all that responsibility. So how are you doing? Your mom said you've had some morning sickness."

"It's nothing. Mom always worries about me. Actually, it's Matthew who's not feeling well tonight. He has a really bad headache."

I had been listening in to the conversation and turned to him. "I'm sorry. Can I get you anything?"

"No, I'm okay," Matthew said, looking embarrassed by the attention. "It's nothing."

"Nothing?" Charlotte said. "On the way here he started driving the wrong way."

I looked at him curiously. "Where were you going?"

Charlotte spoke before he could. "He was headed north on Twenty-third, up towards the old house."

I looked at him and our eyes met. "Are you feeling okay now?"

"I'm feeling better."

"Good." I took a drink of wine and looked away. A few minutes later I said, "Kevin and I have a little gift for you all."

"Honey, I thought we were going to wait until after dinner," Kevin said.

"I'm sorry, I thought it might be fun to mix it up a little. Is that okay?"

He smiled. "Of course. Whatever you please, princess."

Kevin was always that way. He not only called me "princess," he treated me like one. He had since our first date.

I walked to our parlor and retrieved four small wrapped packages and brought them back to the dining room. I handed one to each of our guests.

"*Muchas gracias,*" Roxanne said. "Wait, I should say *grazie.*"

"*Prego,*" I said.

"Ooh, it feels like a CD," Charlotte said. "Wonder what it is."

"Only one way to find out," Kevin said. "Open it."

Roxanne opened hers first. "Oh, shut up. Josh Groban!"

I laughed. "I love that you're so easy to buy for."

Ray was next. "The Grateful Dead, niiiice. Jerry Garcia lives on."

"You got him pegged," Roxanne said.

"I'm not psychic," I said to Ray. "Rox told me what to get you."

"My turn," Charlotte said. She carefully unwrapped her gift. "Oh, Michael Bublé. I love his music. Thanks, Mom and Dad."

"You're welcome, honey," I said.

Roxanne said, "Okay, Matt, it's just you."

I had been watching Matthew out of the corner of my eye. He had just been sitting quietly watching everyone else open their gifts.

"Hey, yours is twice as big as ours," Charlotte said. "Feeling special?"

"I was torn between two CD's," I said. "So I got him both."

"Thanks," Matthew said. He slowly unwrapped the box and lifted out the first CD. He started laughing, then lifted it for us all to see.

"Holy cow," Roxanne said, "I haven't seen that since Ray and I were face-sucking in the back of his Galaxy at the Olympus Drive-in."

"Saturday Night Fever," Matthew said. "Fantastic."

Charlotte started laughing, "Was that a white elephant gift?"

Roxanne piped up, "You're talking about the Bee Gees, girl. Speak with reverence."

Matthew looked at me and smiled. "The Bee Gees. Perfect. Thank you."

"I just didn't want you to go through life not knowing who they were."

He looked at me and there was a sparkle in his eyes. "How could I forget?"

"What's the other one?" Rox asked. "Don't leave us hanging."

Matthew lifted it out of the box, though we saw the smile on his face before the CD. "Savage Garden," he said.

"Oh, that's a good one," Charlotte said. "You like them, don't you," she said to Matthew.

He nodded. "Love them."

"There's a song on there that I especially like," I said. " 'Truly Madly Deeply.' "

"Oh, I just love that song," Charlotte said. "I knew how hip Mom was when she brought home the CD before my friends and I did. I think she got it the day it came out." She turned to me. "I remember once you were playing that song in your bedroom and I walked in on you and you were crying."

I looked down, a little embarrassed. "It's a sweet song."

Matthew nodded. "It brings back memories."

"What kind of memories?" I asked.

He looked into my eyes. "Fond memories."

The conversation suddenly fell into silence. Kevin exhaled. "Okay, okay, I wasn't going to do this until after dinner, but since Beth has opened the floodgates, I have a little surprise too."

I turned and looked at him. "A surprise?"

"Yep, I know you hate surprises, but this time you'll just have to suffer through it." He lifted a flat, beautifully wrapped package he had kept on the ground next to his chair. He handed it to me and kissed me. "Merry Christmas, darling."

"You totally surprised me. I had no idea."

"Listen up, everyone," Kevin said, lifting his hands into the air. "I want you to witness this. For once, I have surprised Beth. You have no idea how hard it is surprising this woman with anything."

"I do," Roxanne said. "The woman's psychic. She can practically predict the future."

"Really?" Matthew asked.

"Last ten Super Bowls and she's five for five on *American Idol*."

"Enough, Rox," I said.

I pulled the ribbon aside, then stripped back the red foil paper. Inside there was a white and green cardboard envelope. I pulled back its flap, exposing its contents. "What's this?" I pulled out two airline tickets. "Fiumicino, Roma."

"Plane tickets to Italy," Kevin said.

For a moment I was speechless. My mind was spinning in a million directions.

Kevin looked at me intently. "Well, is this a happy surprise?"

I leaned over and kissed him. "Very happy. Thank you, sweetheart. You're way too extravagant."

Kevin beamed. "Not for my girl. Merry Christmas, sweetheart."

"I'm so happy for you two," Charlotte said. "Mom hasn't been to Italy since . . . Mr. Matthew." She looked at me. "Wow. It's been a long time since I said that name."

"Who's Mr. Matthew?" Kevin asked.

"Old flame," Roxanne said, waving a hand at him, "Long extinguished, poof, smoke's gone, vanished, no need to worry about him."

"You never told me about a *Mr. Matthew*," Kevin said to me lightly, raising an eyebrow.

"Well, a girl has to keep some secrets," I said, avoiding Matthew's gaze. "It keeps her interesting."

Kevin leaned over and kissed me. "Just the way I like you."

"Mom," Charlotte said, "didn't you throw a coin into the Trevi Fountain?"

"I saw that movie," Roxanne said, *"Three Coins in the Fountain*. If you throw a coin in the Trevi Fountain, you will return to Rome. If you throw two . . ." She stopped. "I don't remember."

"You will find love," Matthew said. He looked at me. "How many coins did you throw, Beth?"

"Two."

"And did you get your wish?"

My eyes welled up with tears and I looked at Kevin. "I got

both of them." I put the tickets back in the envelope. "Thank you."

"You're so romantic, Dad," Charlotte said. "Just like Matthew."

"Well," he said, grinning like a Cheshire cat, "did anyone happen to notice the date on those tickets?"

He looked at me and I shook my head.

"We're leaving the day after tomorrow. We're spending New Year's Eve in the Piazza del Popolo." He turned to Charlotte and Matthew. "And by 'we' I mean the four of us. We need to go before our baby girl gets too far along with her own baby."

Charlotte screamed. "Really?!" She got up and walked around the table to Kevin and hugged him. "Thank you, Daddy."

He beamed with joy. "You're welcome, sweetheart."

"Thank you, Kevin," Matthew said. "That's very generous."

"Well, I thought it might be a nice getaway while it's still just the four of us. Kind of a last hurrah of the empty nesters. And besides," he said, winking, "this way I don't have to hire an interpreter."

"Thank you, darling," I said to Kevin. "It's a wonderful surprise."

He raised a glass. "A toast. To family."

"To family," I said. "And that includes you, Rox."

"Darn right," she said. "So how 'bout it, Kev? You springing for us too?"

"Next time," he said.

"The story of my life." She raised her glass. "To family."

"To family," Matthew said.

I took a drink of wine, then slowly panned the room. It was perfect. There was so much joy and warmth. There was so much to be grateful for. Everyone was so happy. Everything was perfect.

When the excitement had died a little, I said, "Matthew, why don't you come with me and I'll get you some Tylenol."

He set his napkin on the table. "Thank you. I'll be right back," he said to Charlotte.

I hurried up the stairs to my bedroom. When Matthew walked into the upstairs hallway, I grabbed his arm and pulled him into my room and shut the door behind us.

"Beth," he said.

I threw my arms around him. "It's been so long."

"It's like it was just this afternoon," Matthew said.

I stepped back. "It's been eighteen years. I look old, don't I?"

He shook his head. "You've never looked more beautiful."

I smiled sadly. "You have no idea what it's been like holding this secret with no one to share it with." I squeezed his hand. "*Mamma mia*, the day Charlotte brought you home for the first time and pretending that we'd never met"—I brushed a tear from my cheek—"then waiting for Charlotte to get sick . . ."

"Charlotte doesn't have cancer," he said, as much a question as a statement.

"No, she doesn't. You came back to save me and you saved her too. You saved all of us."

"How long have you been married to Kevin?"

"Thirteen years."

"Do you love him?"

"With all my heart. He's a wonderful man. And I have you to thank for him."

"Me?"

"After Marc, I didn't think I could ever trust a man again. You gave me the courage to trust. You gave me hope that there were men out there like you."

He put his hand on my cheek and I reached up and put my hand on his. "So what do we do now?" he asked.

A broad smile crossed my face. "We live. You have Charlotte back. I have Kevin. We've been blessed."

"And us?"

I shook my head and smiled. "I'm grateful that my daughter has a man like you. Two of my favorite people in the world have each other. What more could a mother want?"

"Is that what you want?"

My eyes filled with tears. "I'll always love you. Do you know that?"

He nodded. "And I'll always love you."

"And we'll always have 1990."

He smiled. "The year Milli Vanilli fell."

I started laughing. "You were right about that."

"You think I would make that up?"

We both laughed. Then he said, "Merry Christmas, Beth."

"Merry Christmas." I just gazed into his eyes for a moment, then said, "We better get back to the party."

He nodded, turned to go, then stopped. "May I hold you just once more?"

I looked at him for a moment, then smiled. "I'd like that."

He stepped into me and put his arms around me. My heart was full. Not with sadness or regret, nor passion or desire, but with love—gratitude and love. Maybe they're the same things. And while he held me, I was twenty-eight again. I'm certain of it. Eighteen years wasn't too long to wait for such a moment.

TELL THE WORLD THIS BOOK WAS		
GOOD	BAD	SO-SO

RICHARD PAUL EVANS is the #1 bestselling author of *The Christmas Box*. His novels have each appeared on the *New York Times* bestseller list; there are more than 14 million copies of his books in print. His books have been translated into more than twenty-five languages and several have been international bestsellers. He has won two first-place Storytelling World Awards for his children's books and the *Romantic Times* Best Women's Novel award. Evans received the *Washington Times* Humanitarian of the Century Award and the Volunteers of America National Empathy Award for his work helping abused children. Evans lives in Salt Lake City, Utah, with his wife, Keri, and their five children.